JESS KEATI

BUNBUN & BONBON

HOPPY GO LUCKY

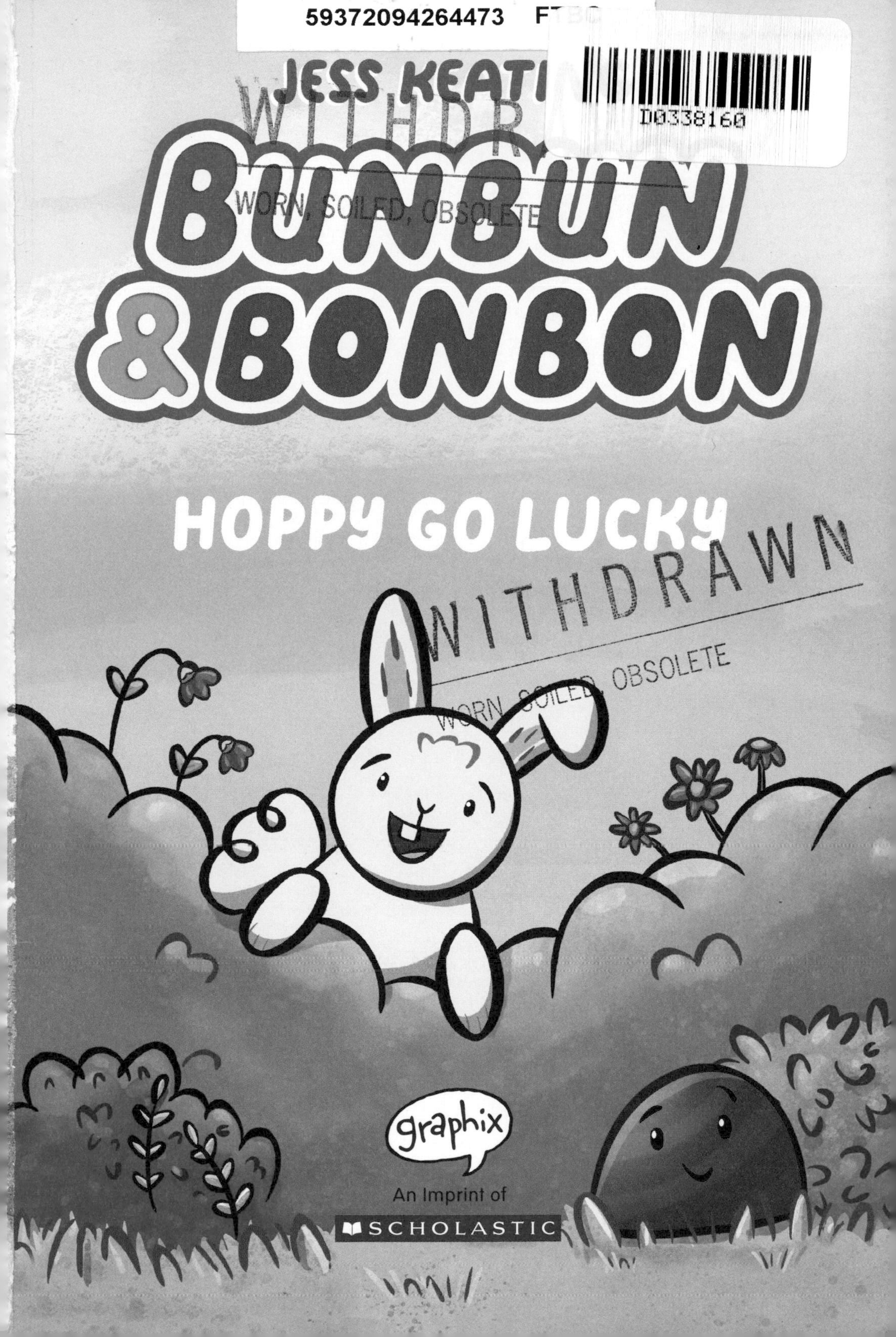

graphix
An Imprint of
SCHOLASTIC

For Justin and Kathleen,
who always look on the sparkly side.

All rights reserved. Published by Graphix, an imprint of Scholastic Inc.,
Publishers since 1920. SCHOLASTIC, GRAPHIX, and associated logos are
trademarks and/or registered trademarks of Scholastic Inc.

The publisher does not have any control over and does not assume any
responsibility for author or third-party websites or their content.

Library of Congress Control Number: 2020937427

ISBN 978-1-338-64686-3 (hardcover)
ISBN 978-1-338-64685-6 (paperback)

10 9 8 7 6 5 4 3 2 1   21 22 23 24 25

Printed in China   62
First edition, January 2021
Edited by Ken Geist and Jonah Newman
Book design by Phil Falco and Steve Ponzo
Color assistance: Wes Dzioba
Creative Director: Phil Falco
Publisher: David Saylor

CONTENTS

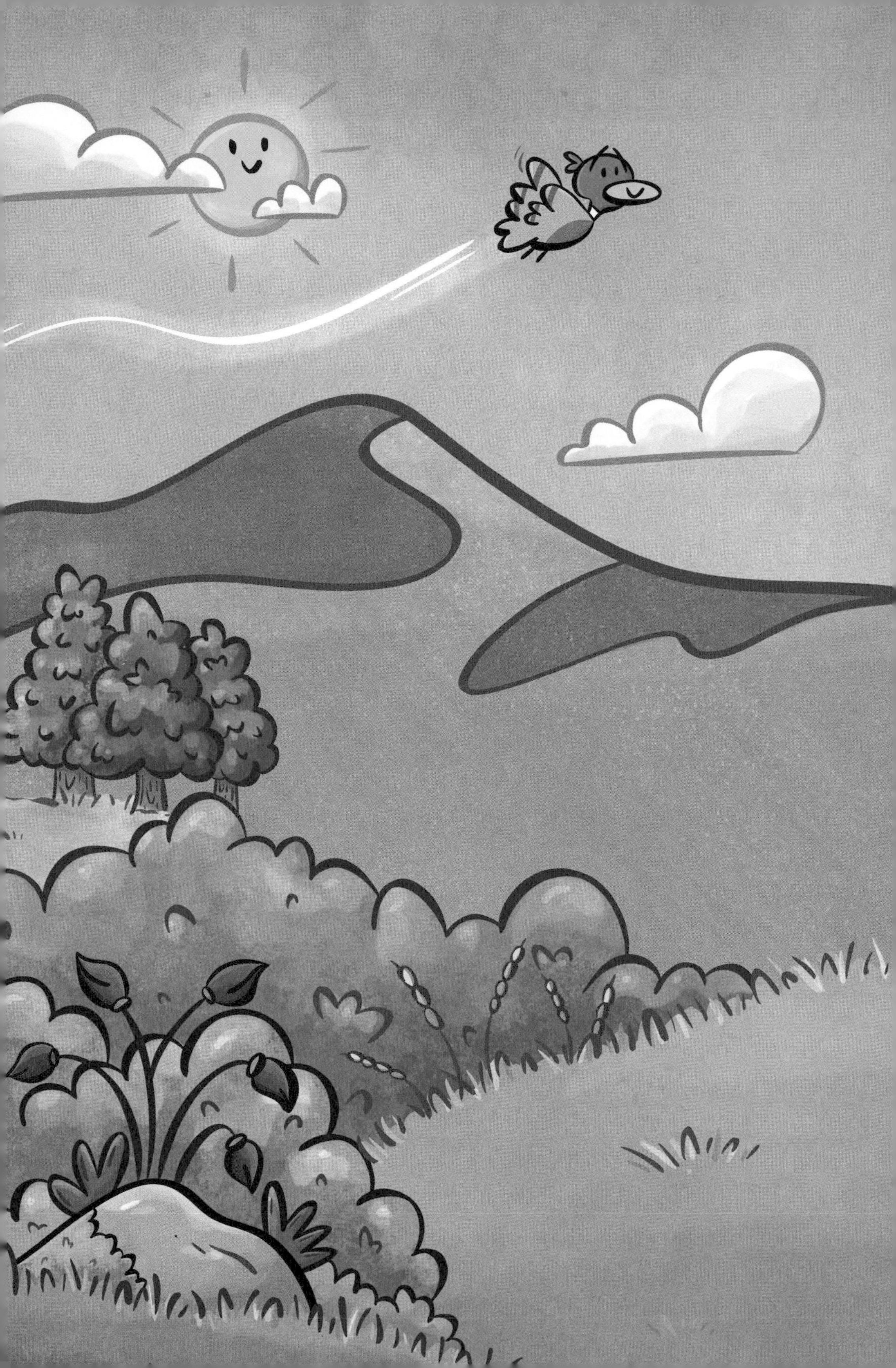

THE BAD LUCK DAY

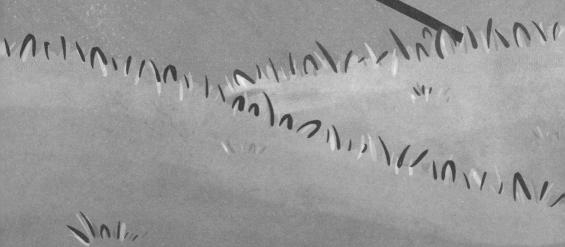

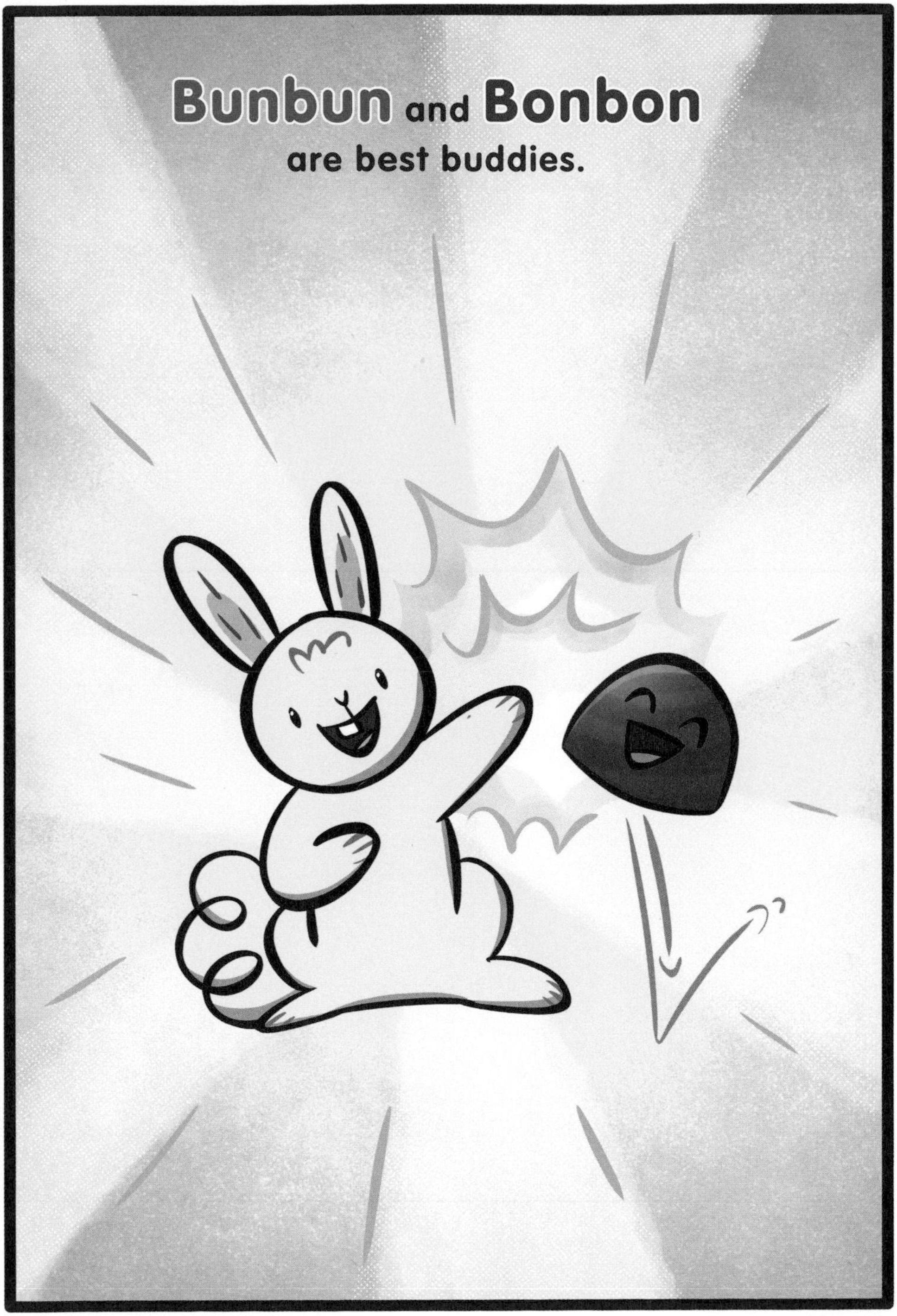
Bunbun and Bonbon
are best buddies.

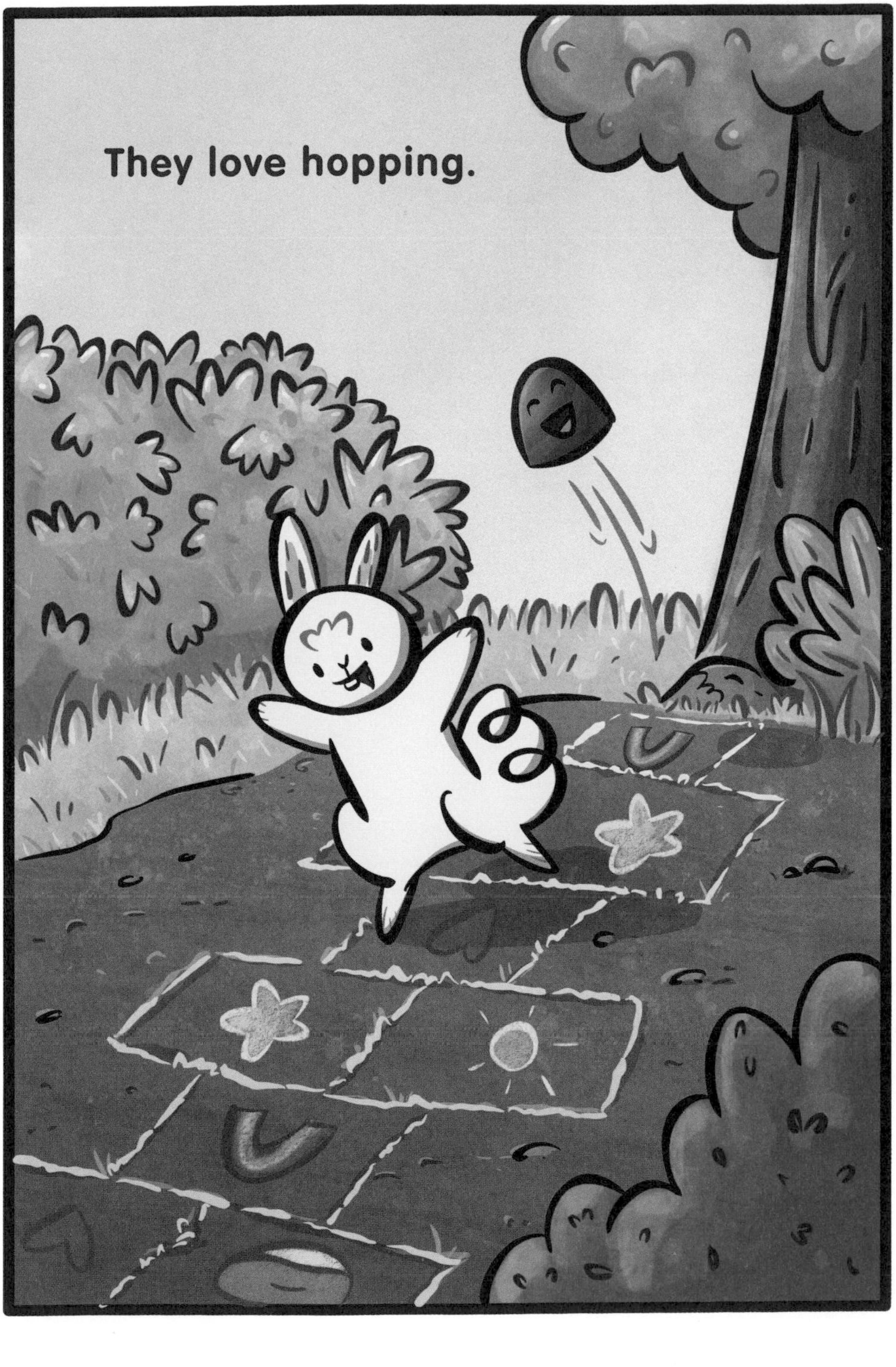
They love hopping.

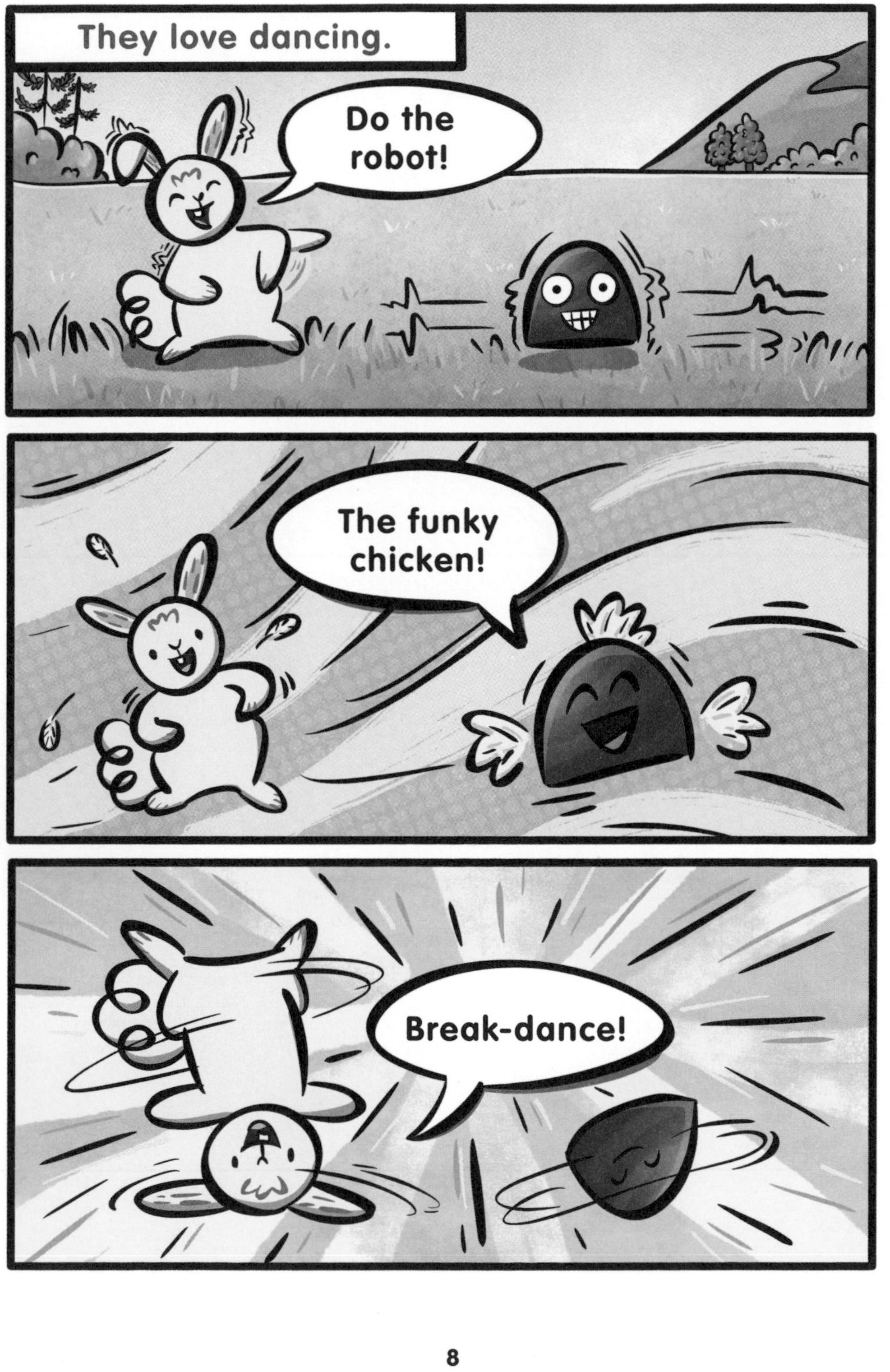
They love dancing.
Do the robot!
The funky chicken!
Break-dance!

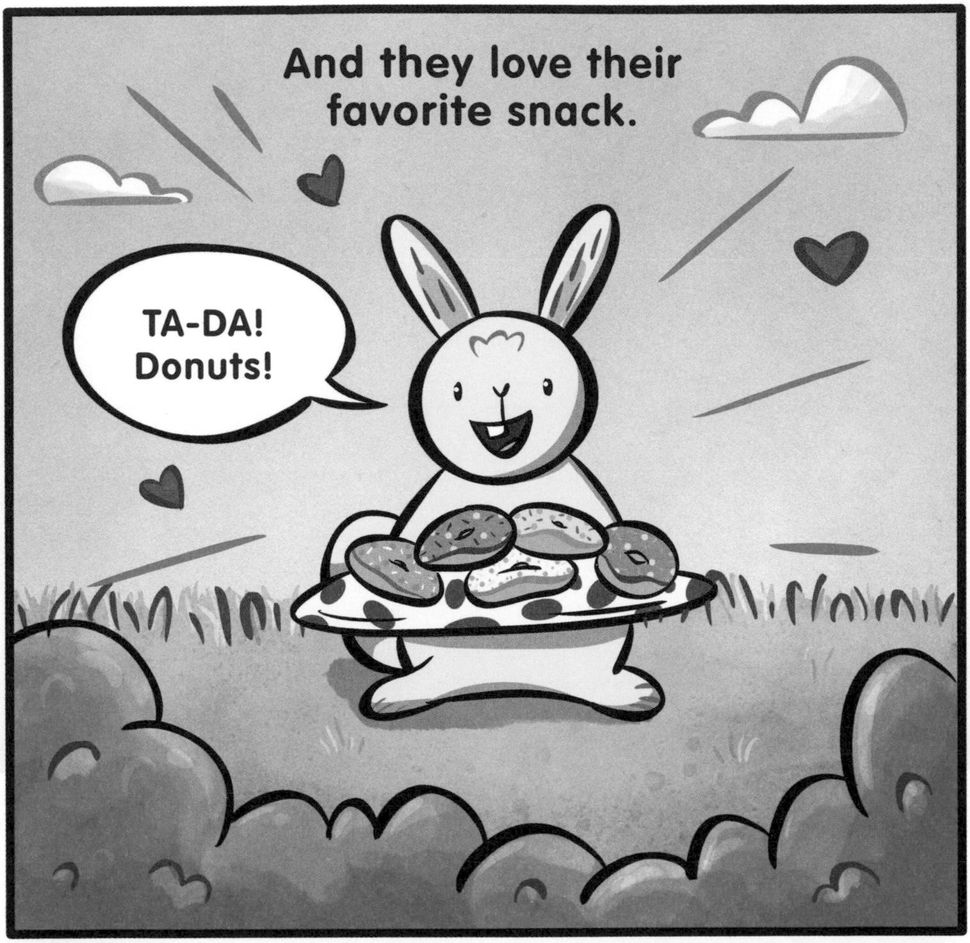
And they love their favorite snack.
TA-DA! Donuts!

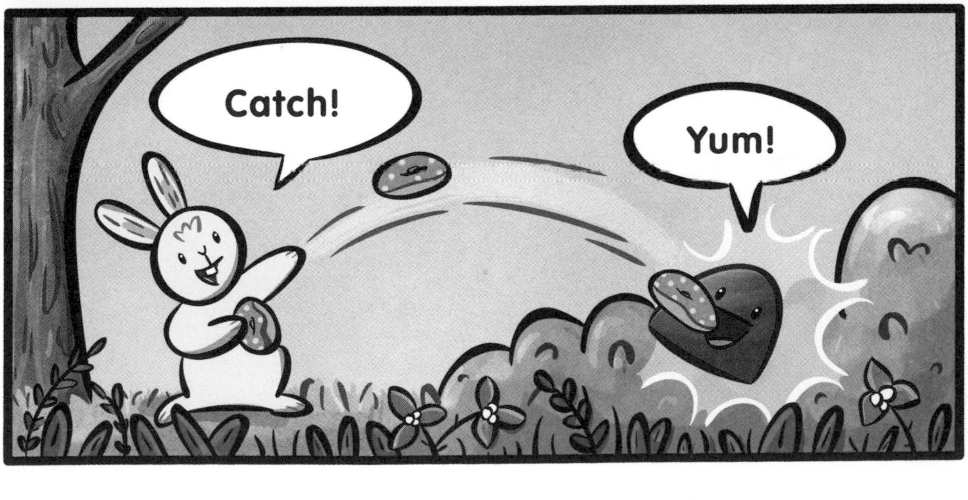
Catch!
Yum!

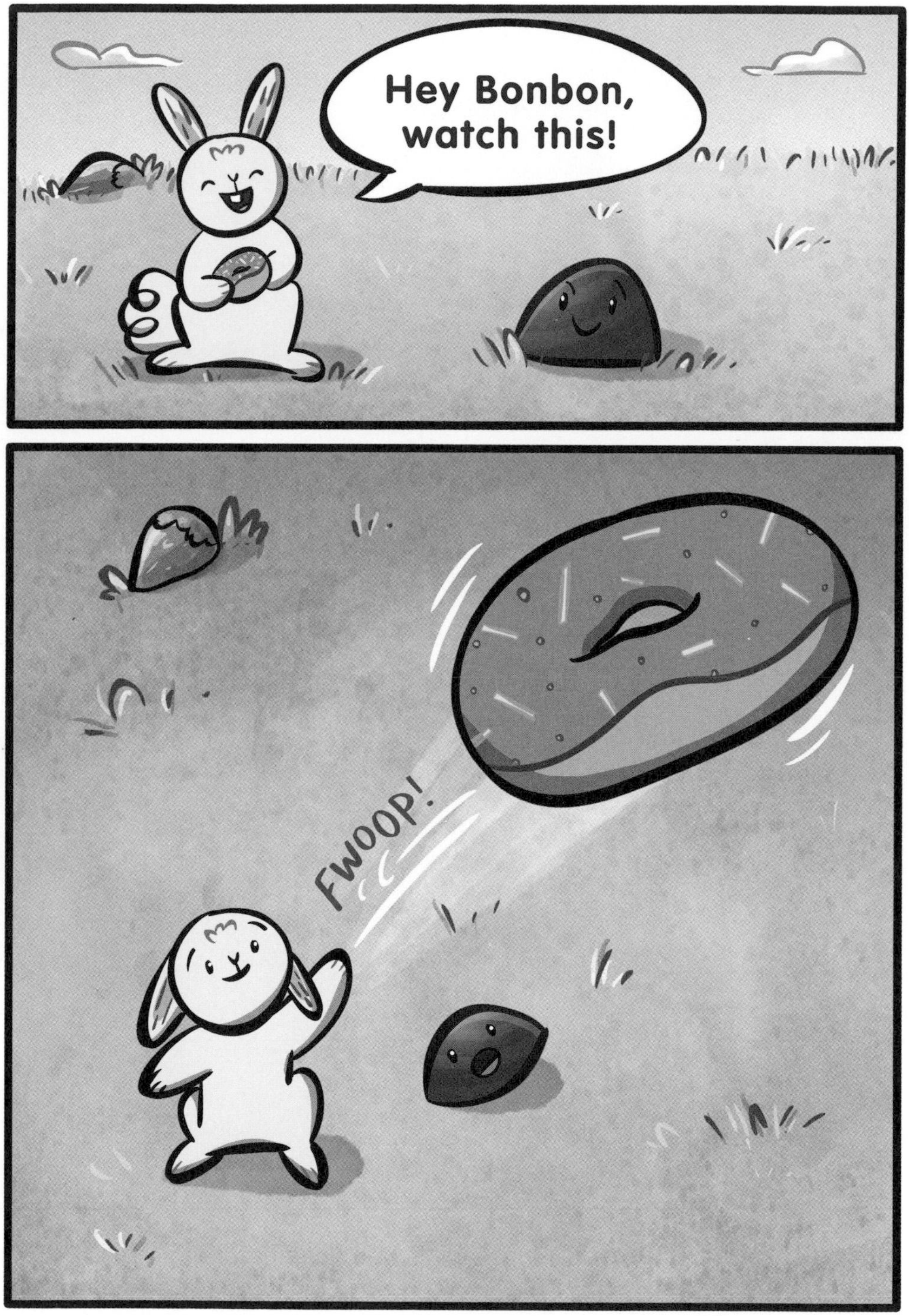
Hey Bonbon, watch this!
FWOOP!

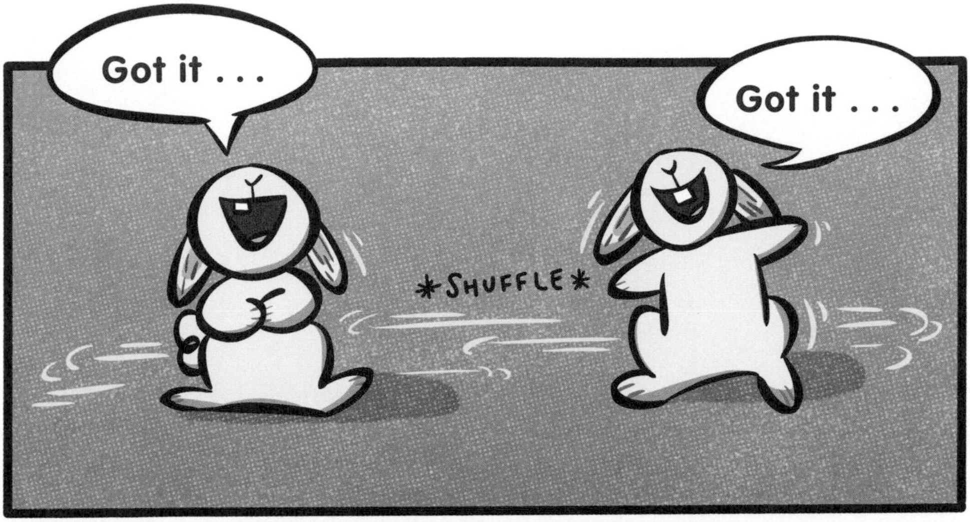
Got it . . .
Got it . . .
SHUFFLE

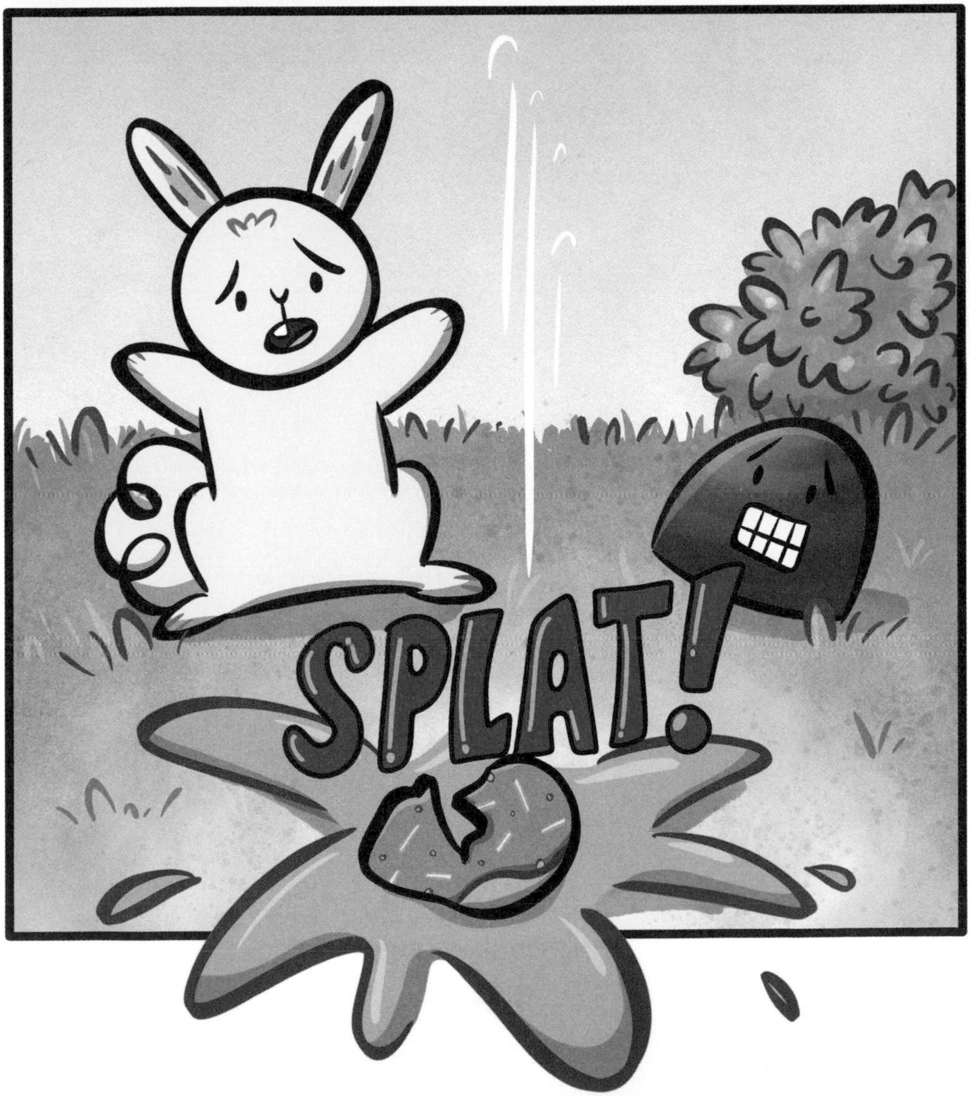
SPLAT!

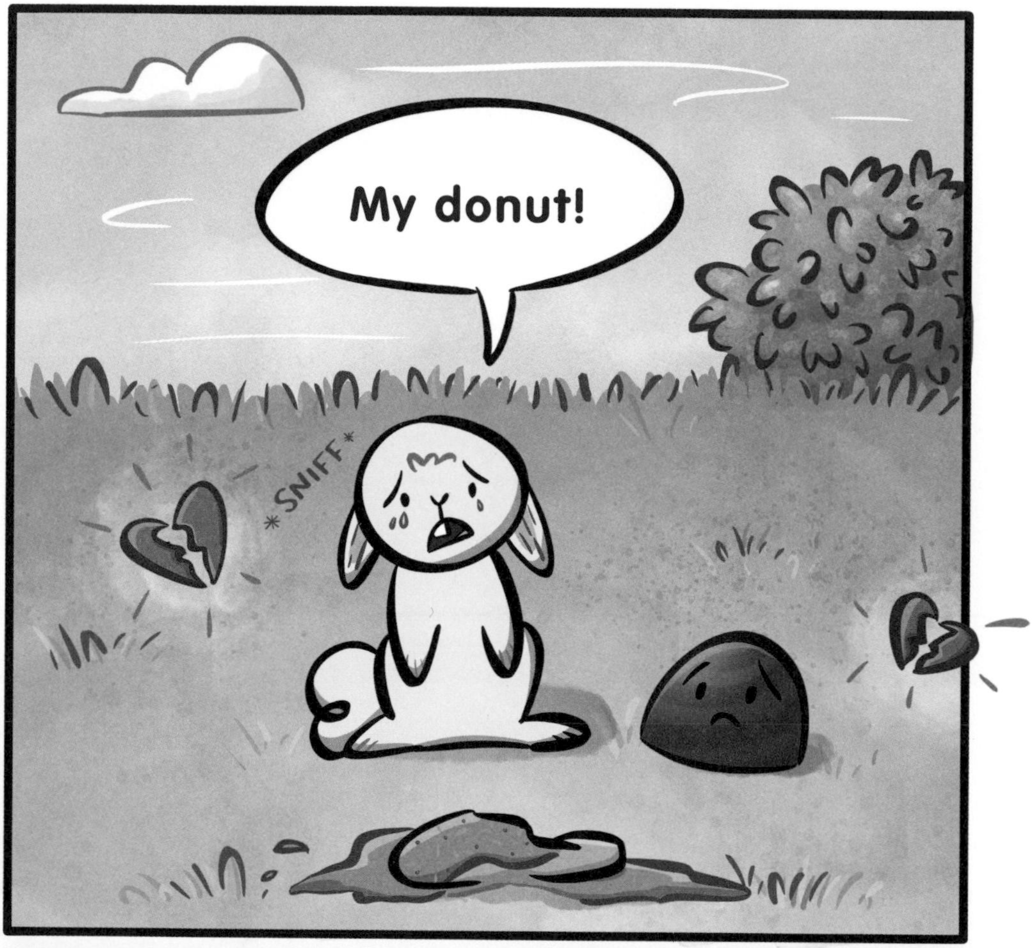
My donut!
SNIFF

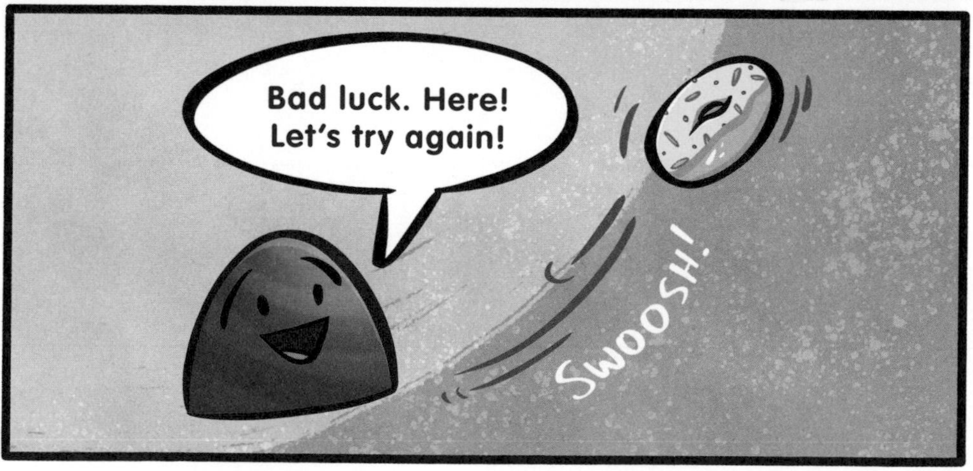
Bad luck. Here!
Let's try again!
SWOOSH!

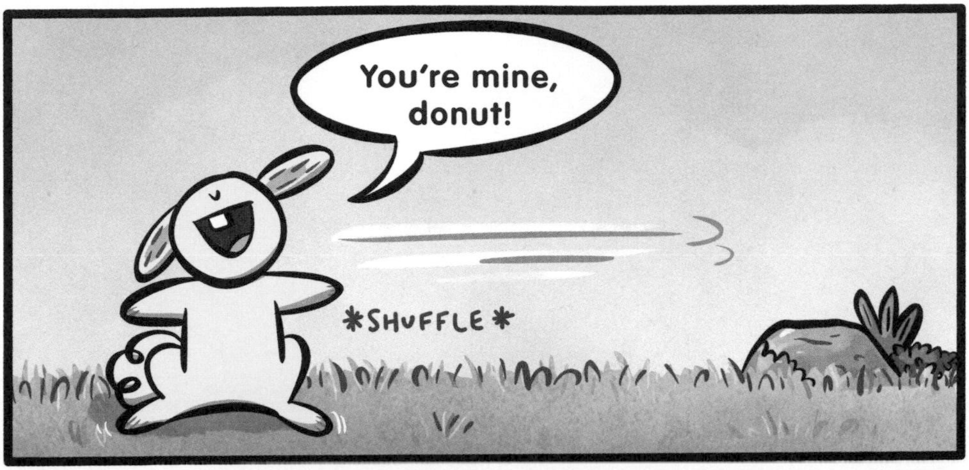
You're mine, donut!
SHUFFLE

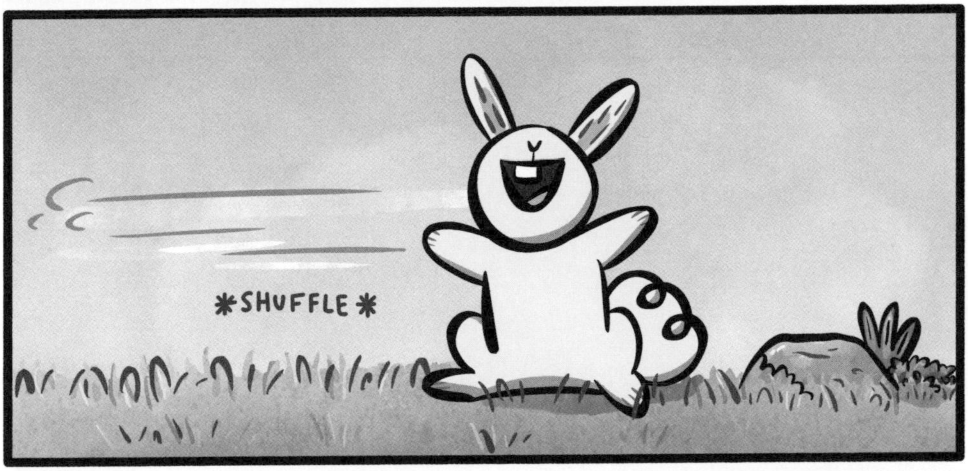
SHUFFLE

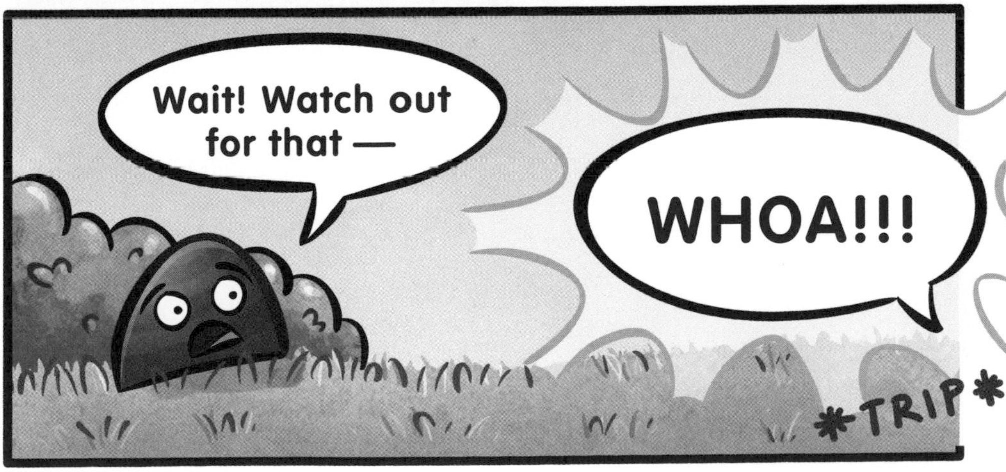
Wait! Watch out for that —
WHOA!!!
TRIP

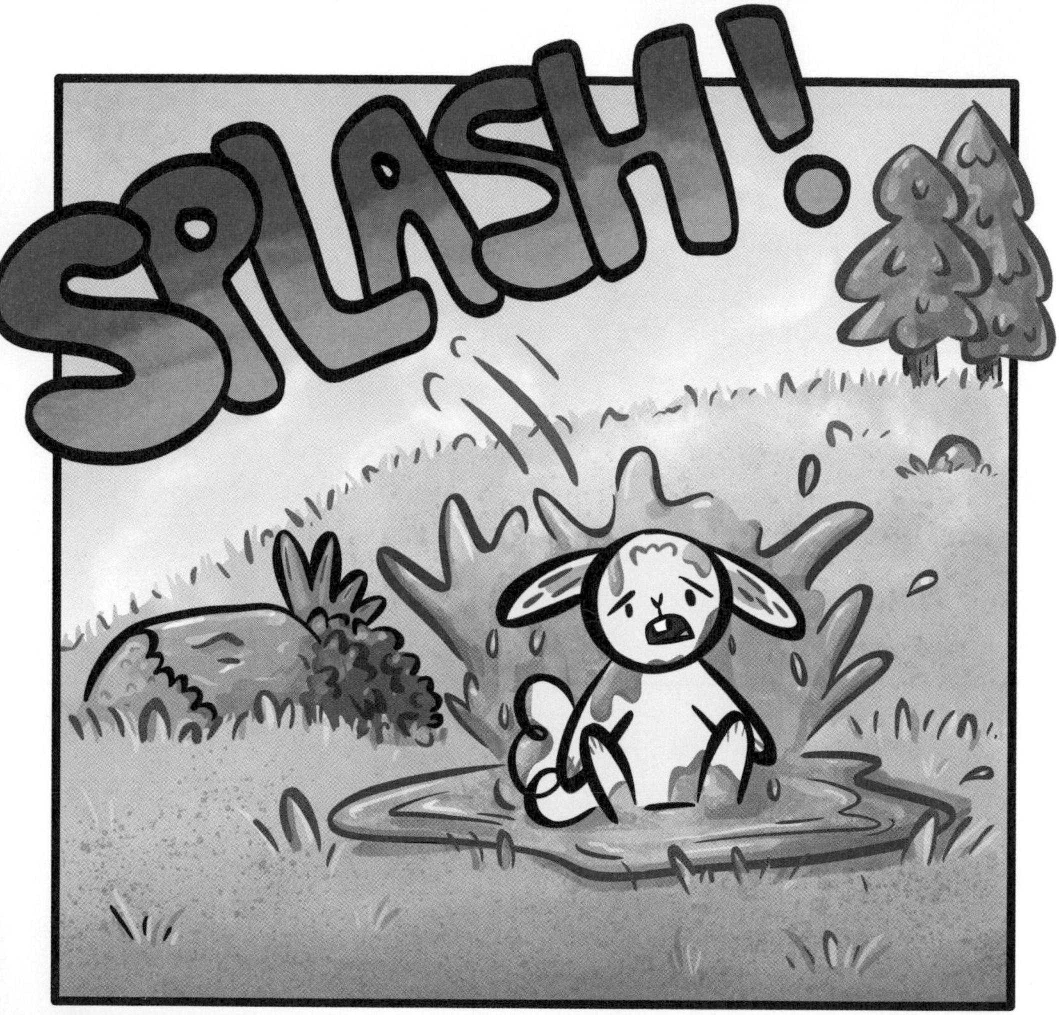
SPLASH!

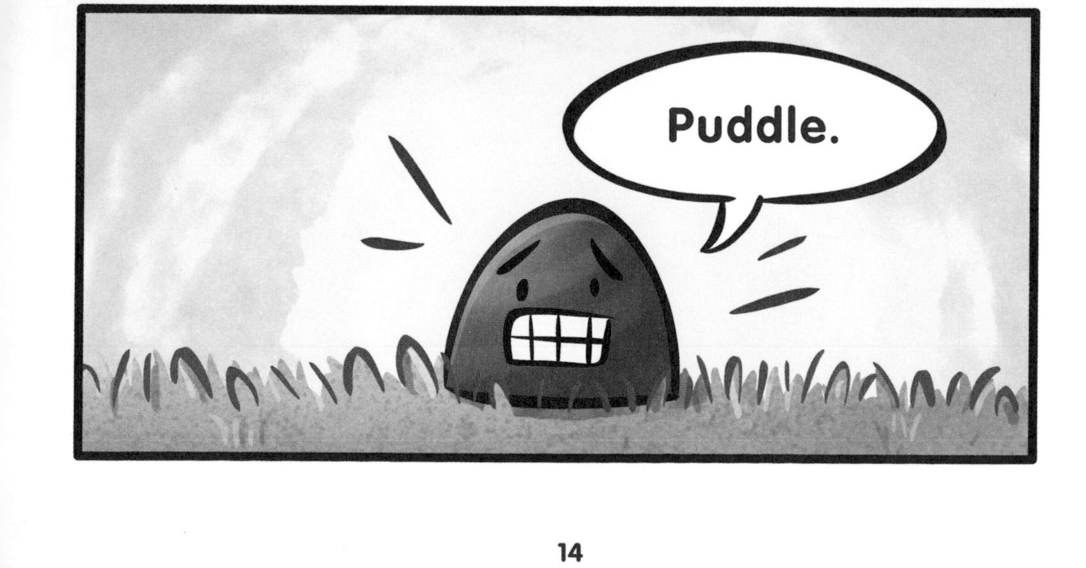
Puddle.

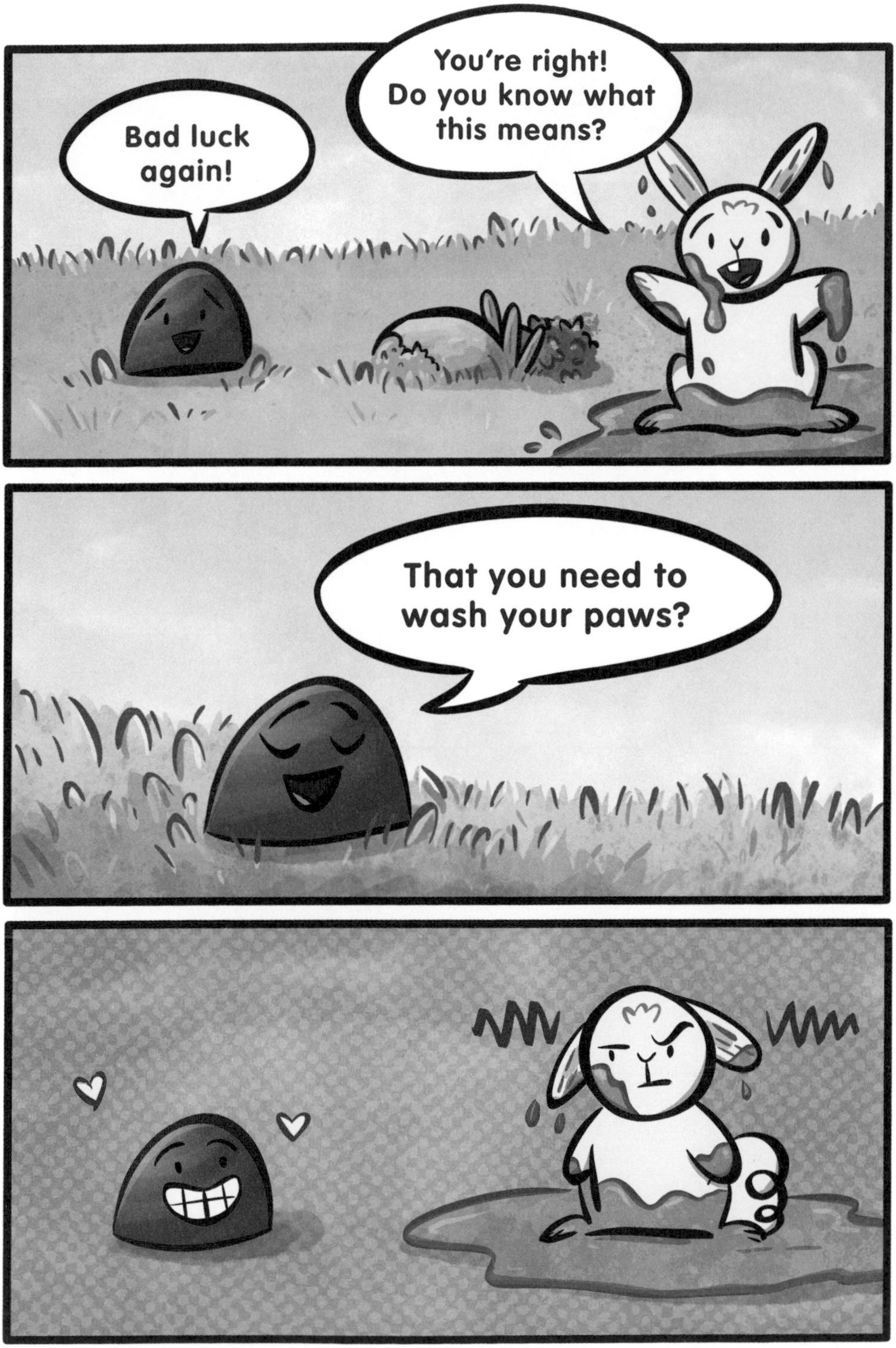
Bad luck again!
You're right! Do you know what this means?
That you need to wash your paws?

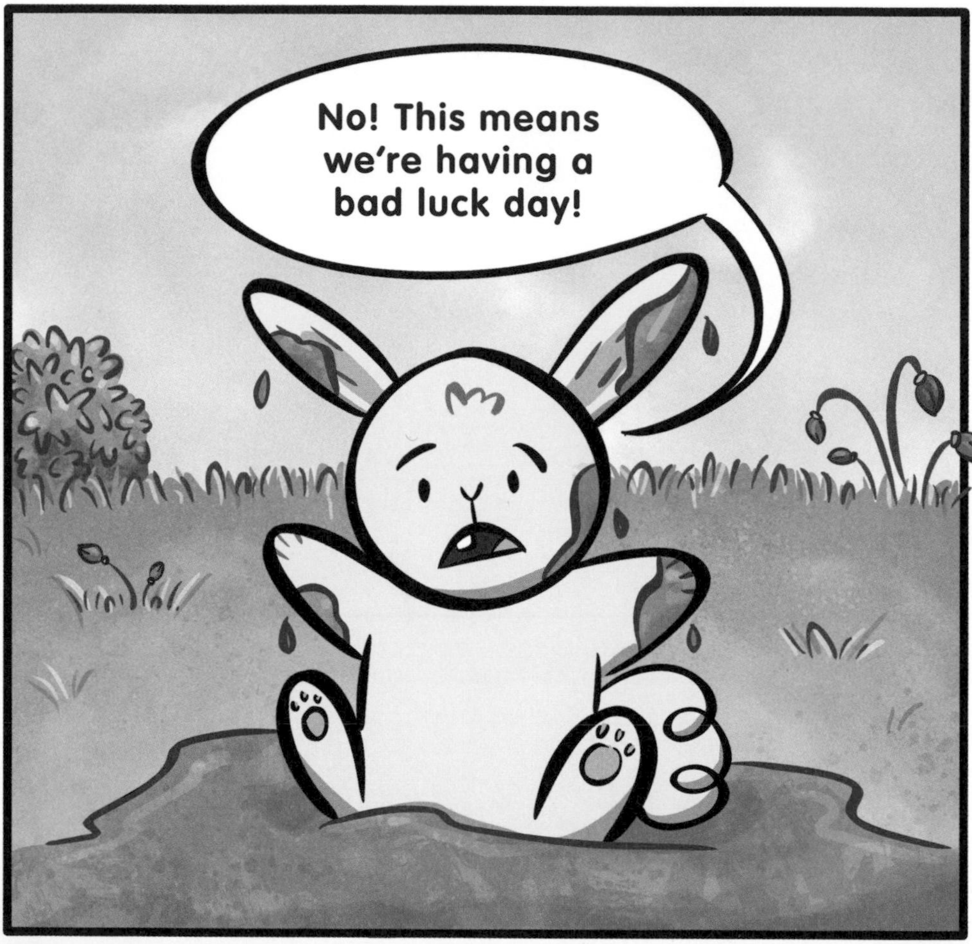
No! This means we're having a bad luck day!

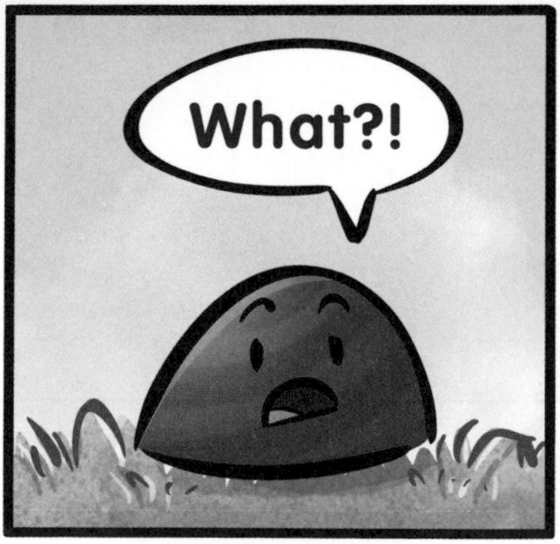
What?!

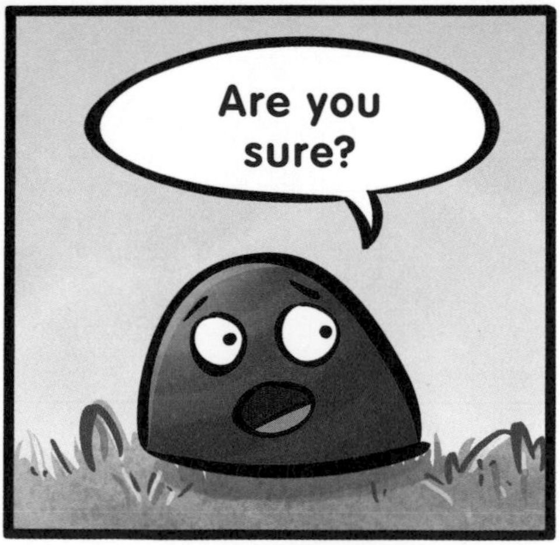
Are you sure?

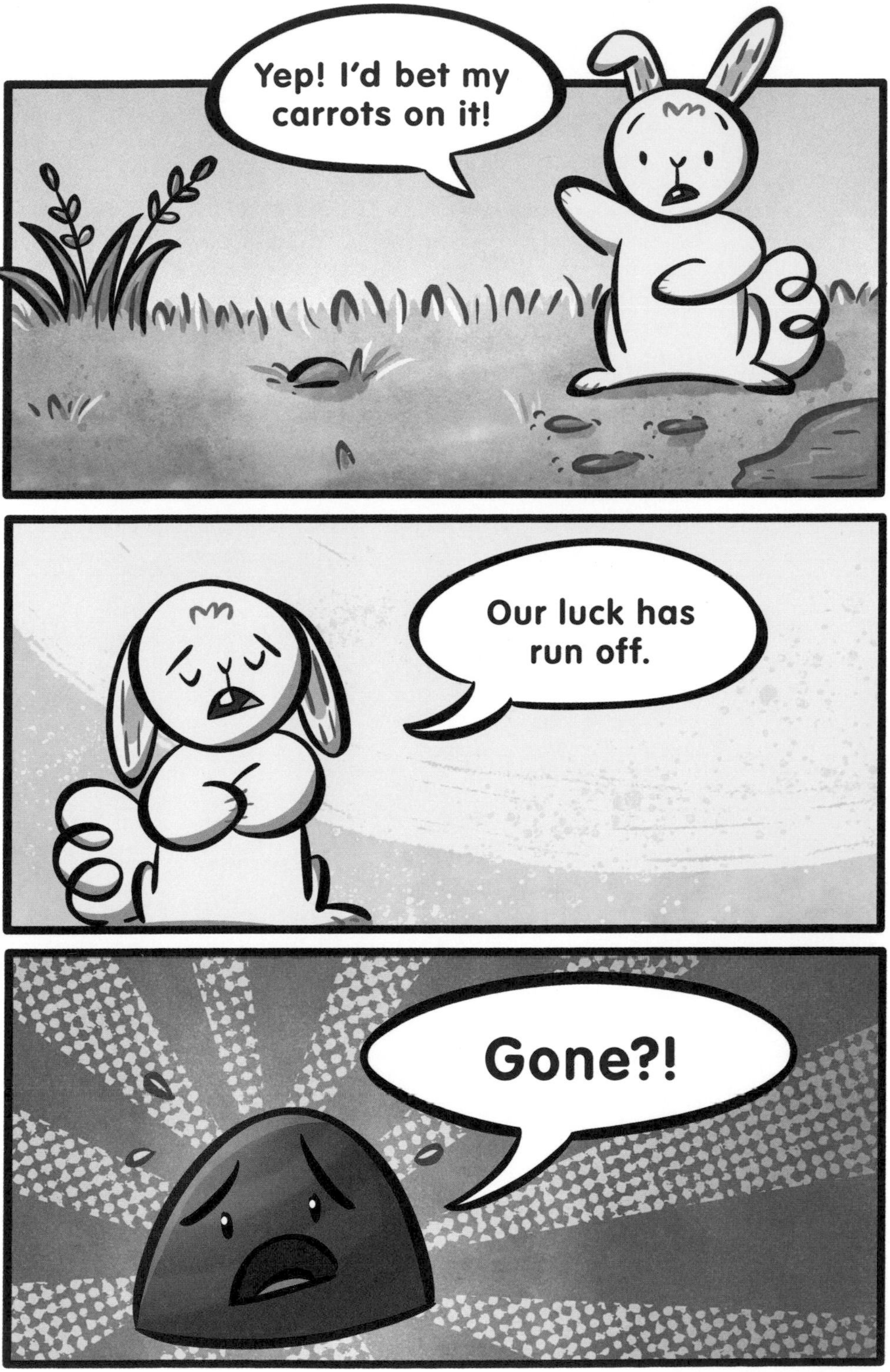
Yep! I'd bet my carrots on it!
Our luck has run off.
Gone?!

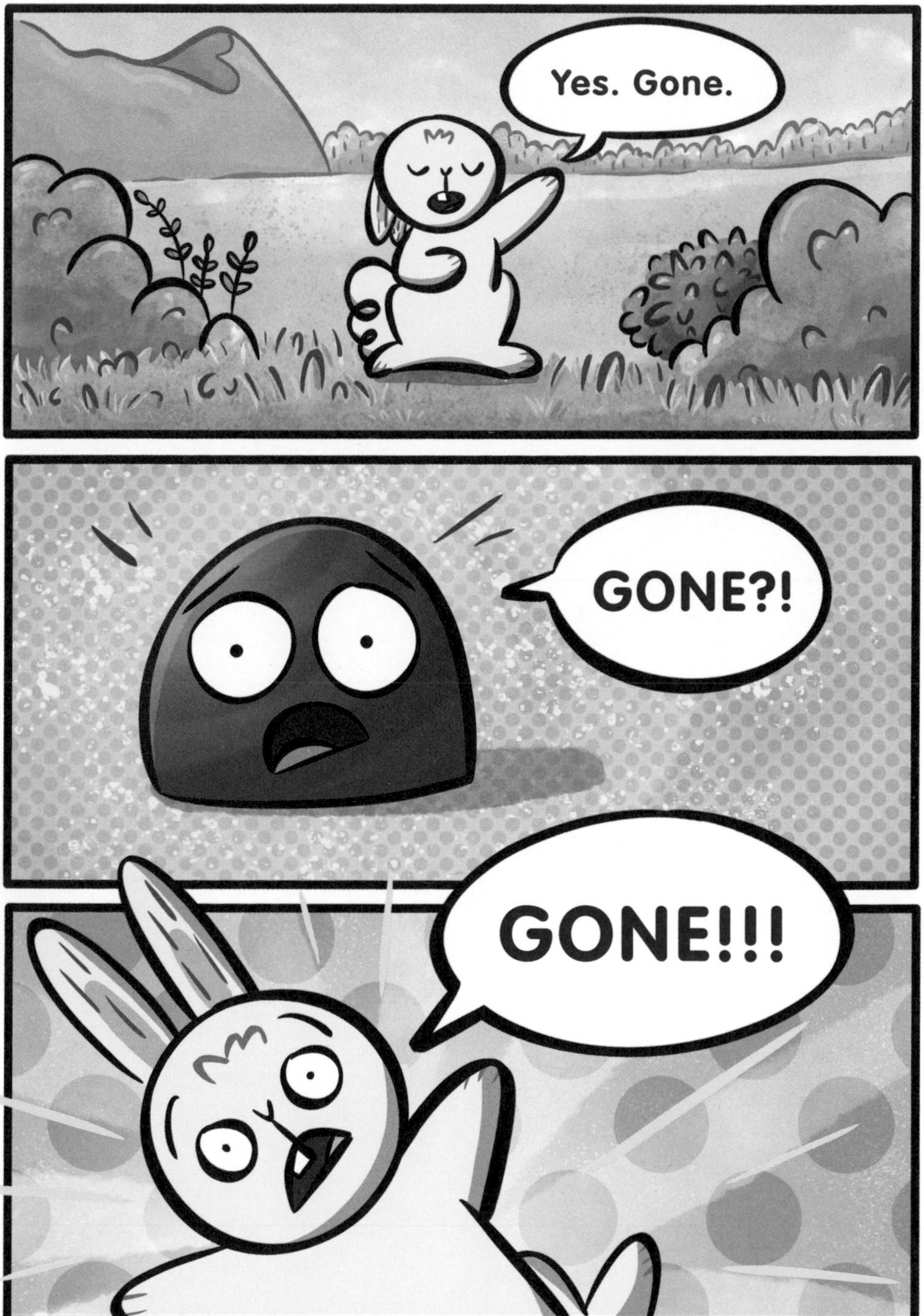
Yes. Gone.
GONE?!
GONE!!!

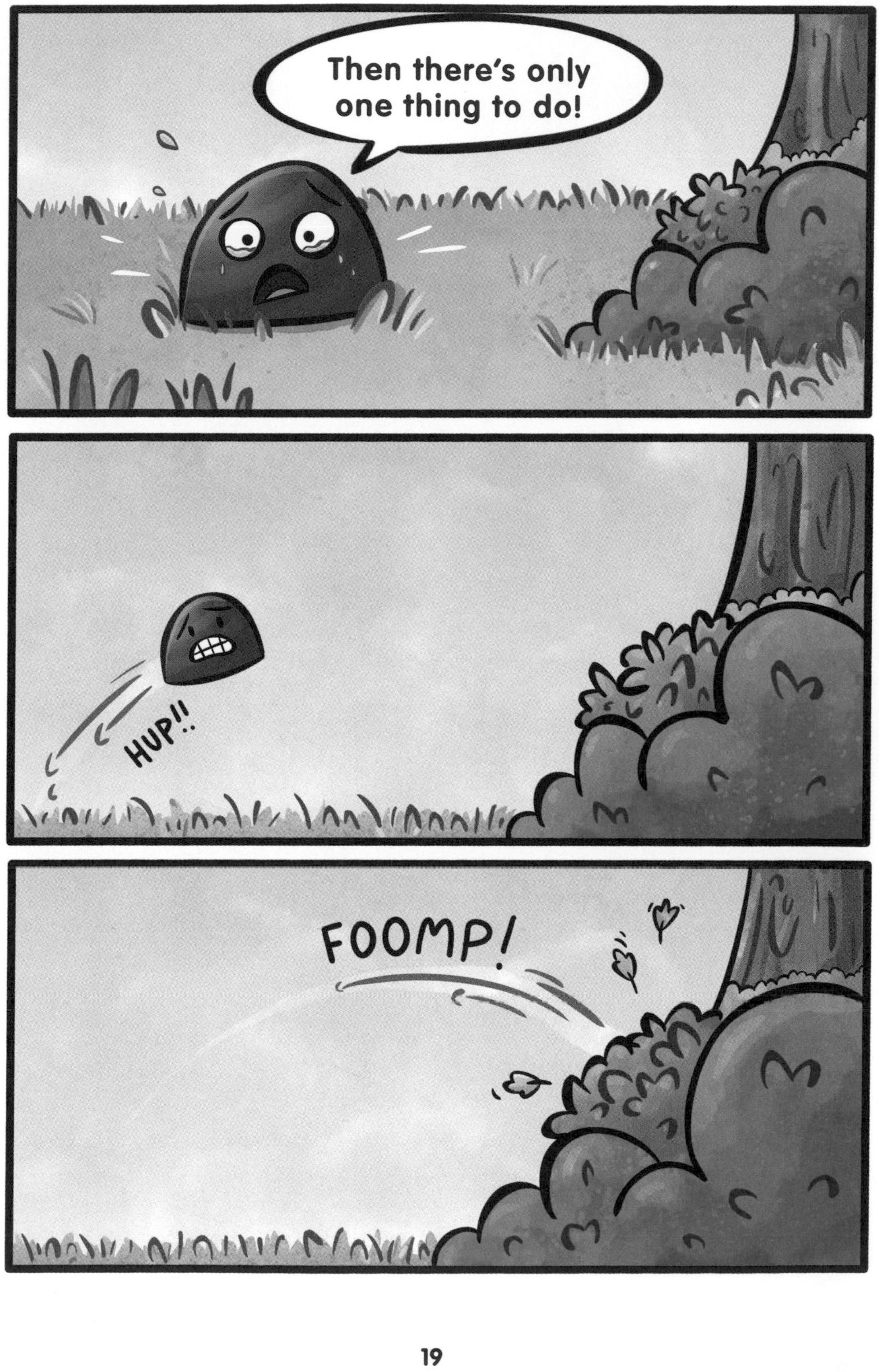
Then there's only one thing to do!
HUP!!
FOOMP!

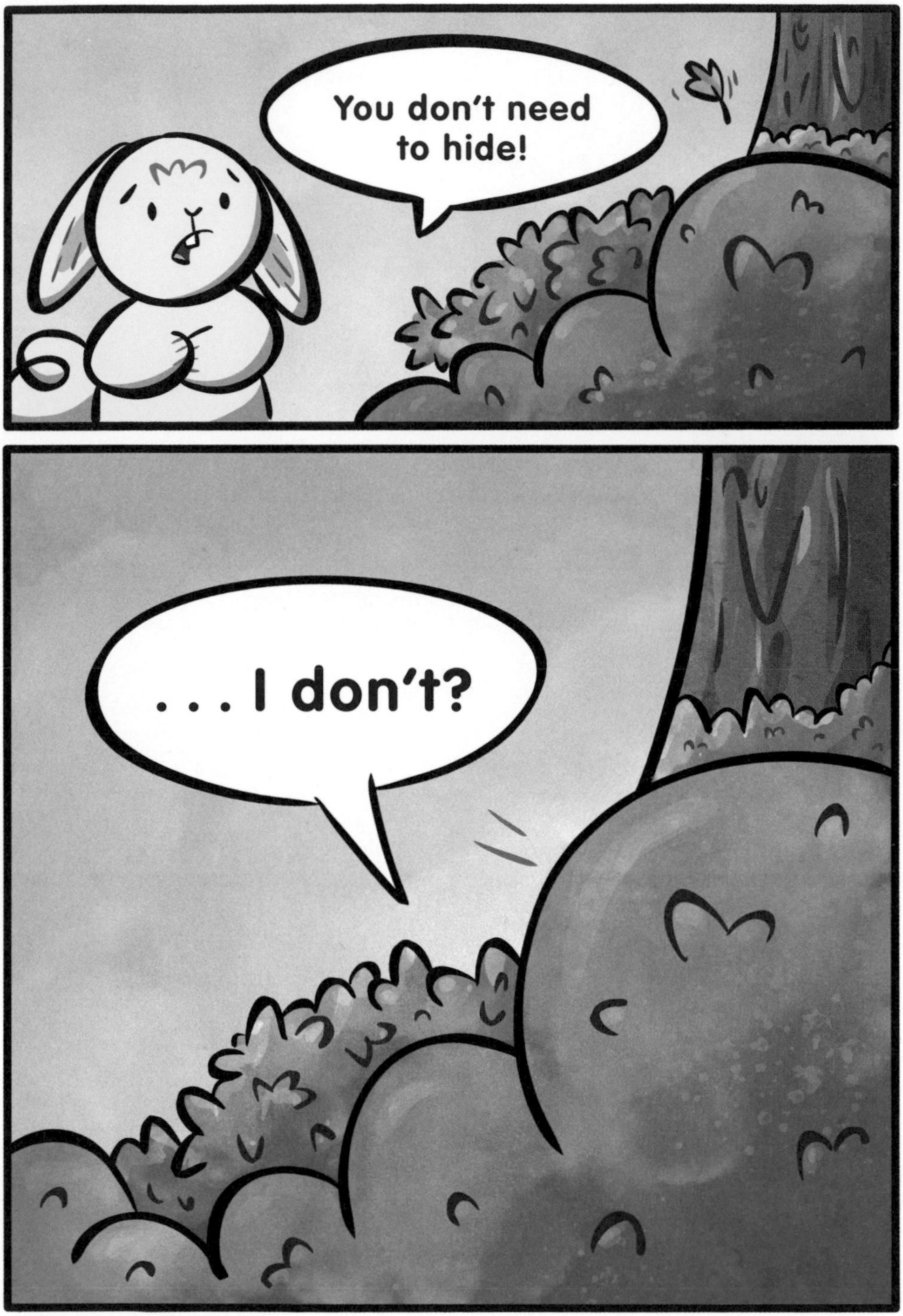
You don't need to hide!
. . . I don't?

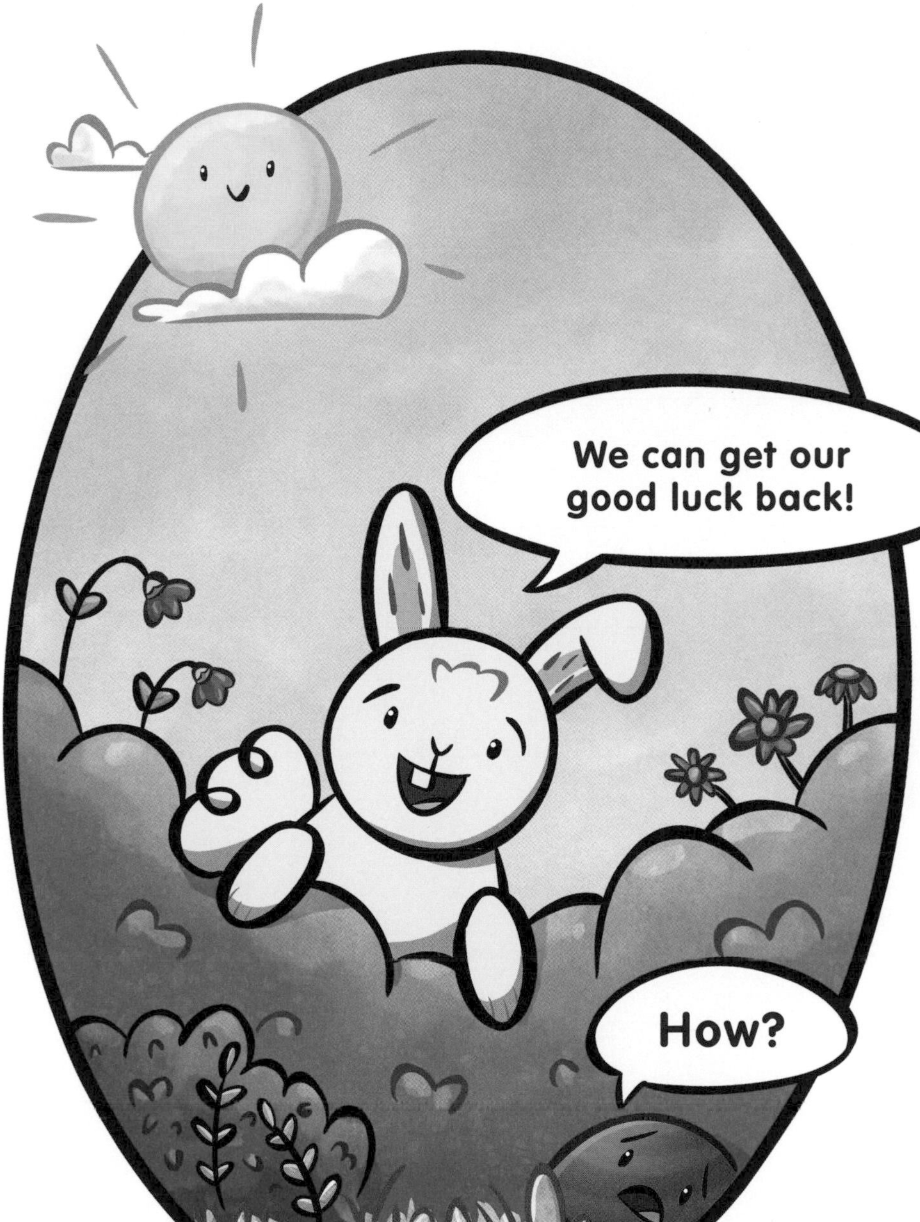
We can get our good luck back!
How?

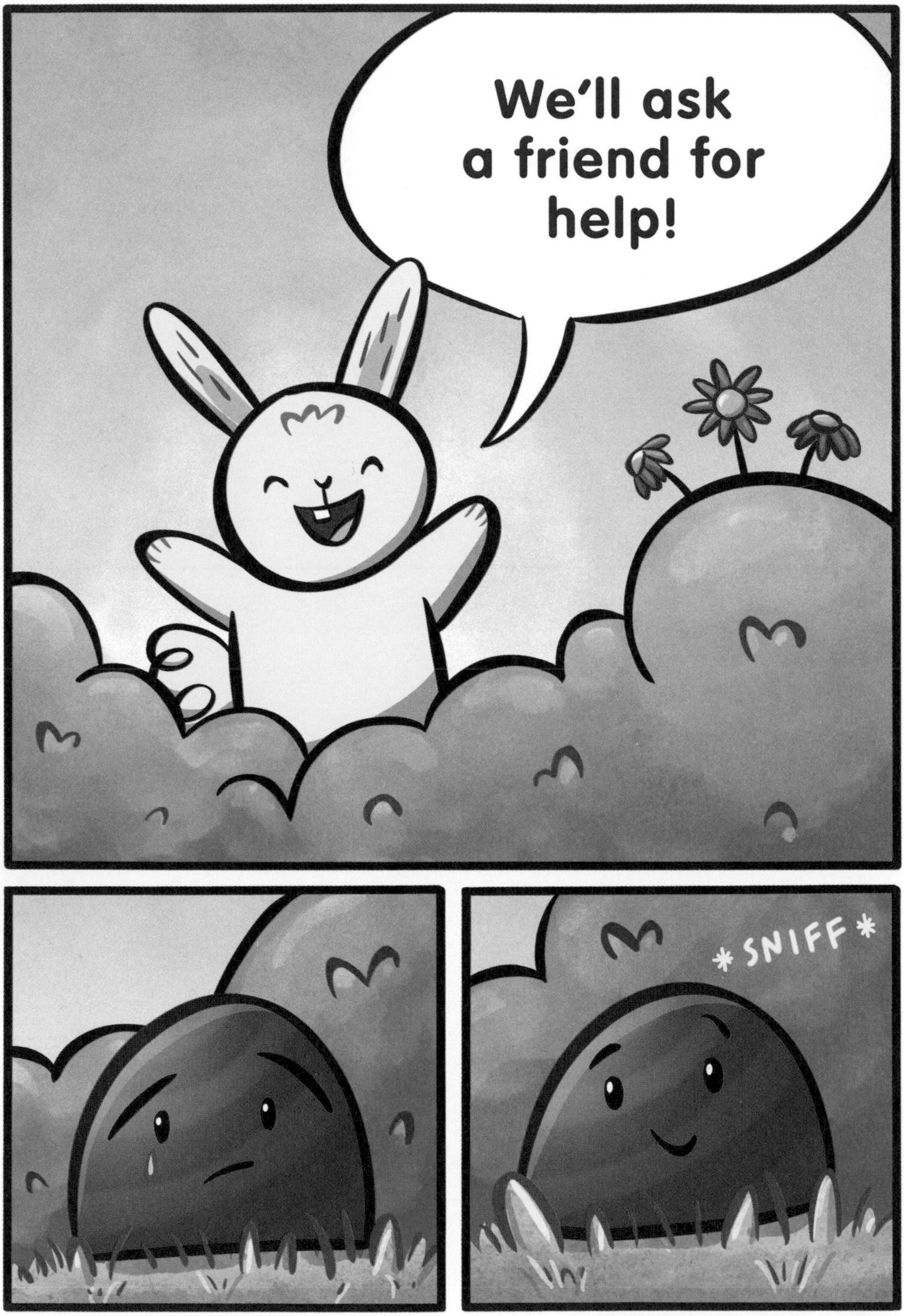
We'll ask a friend for help!
SNIFF

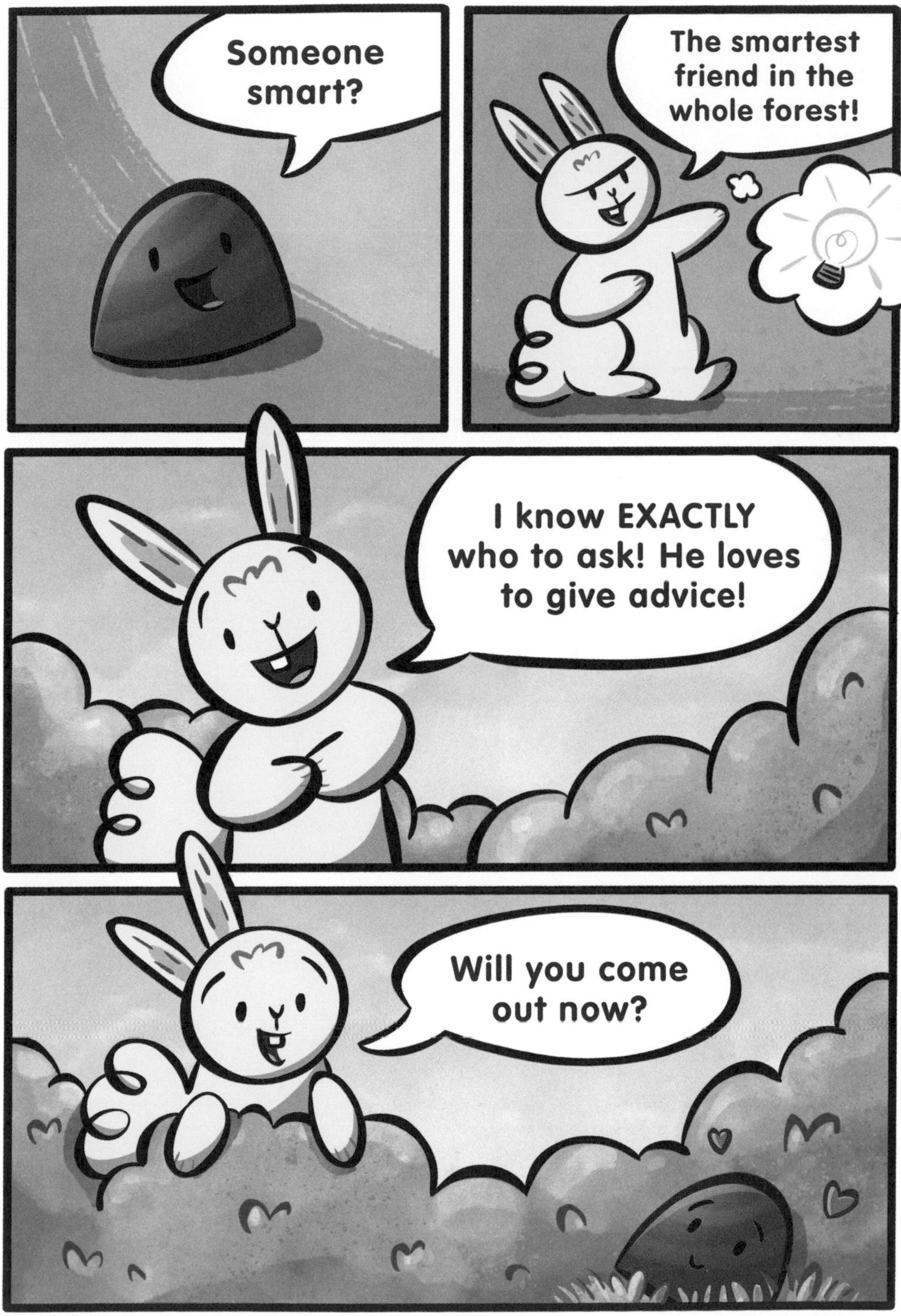
Someone smart?
The smartest friend in the whole forest!
I know EXACTLY who to ask! He loves to give advice!
Will you come out now?

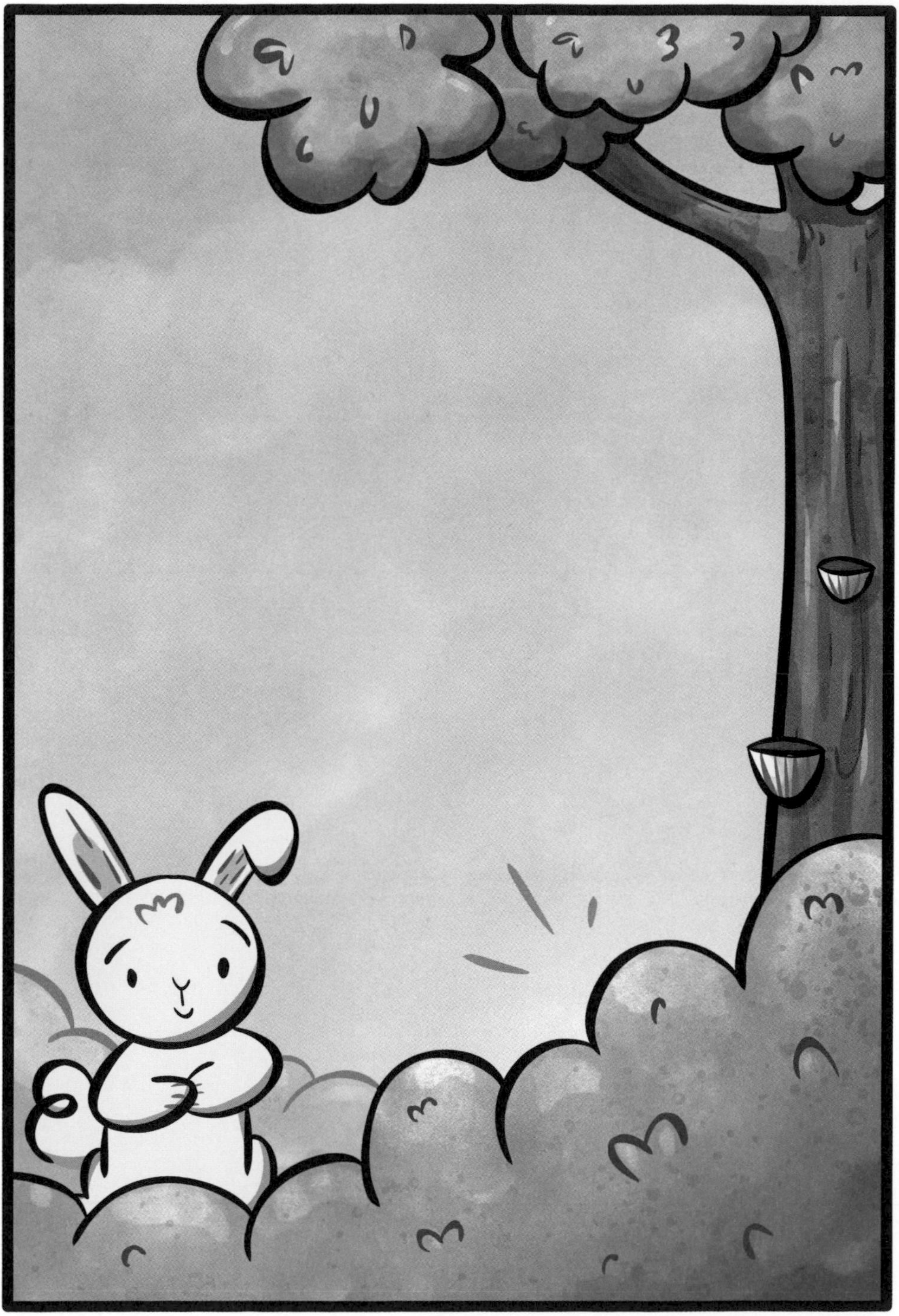

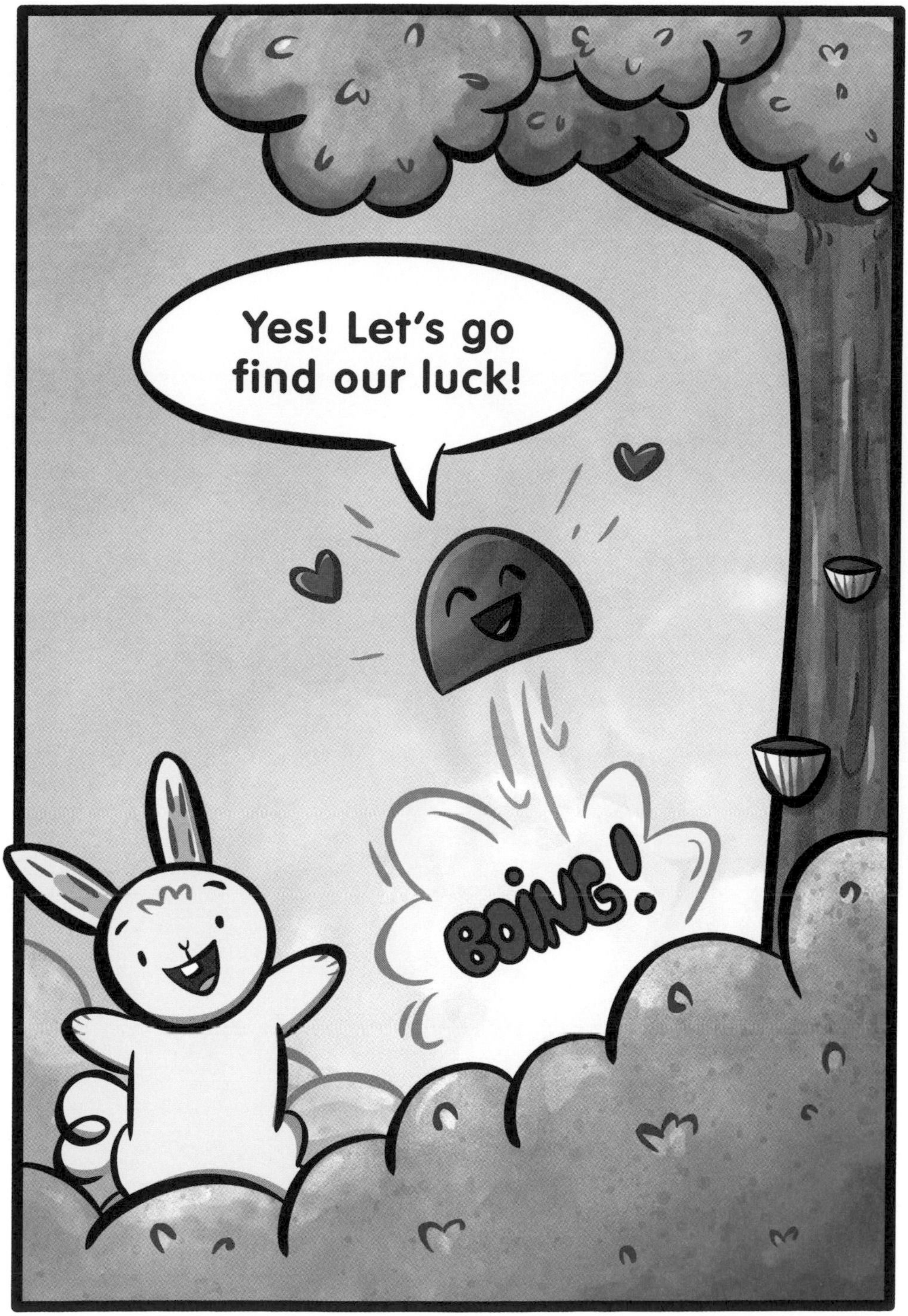
Yes! Let's go find our luck!
BOING!

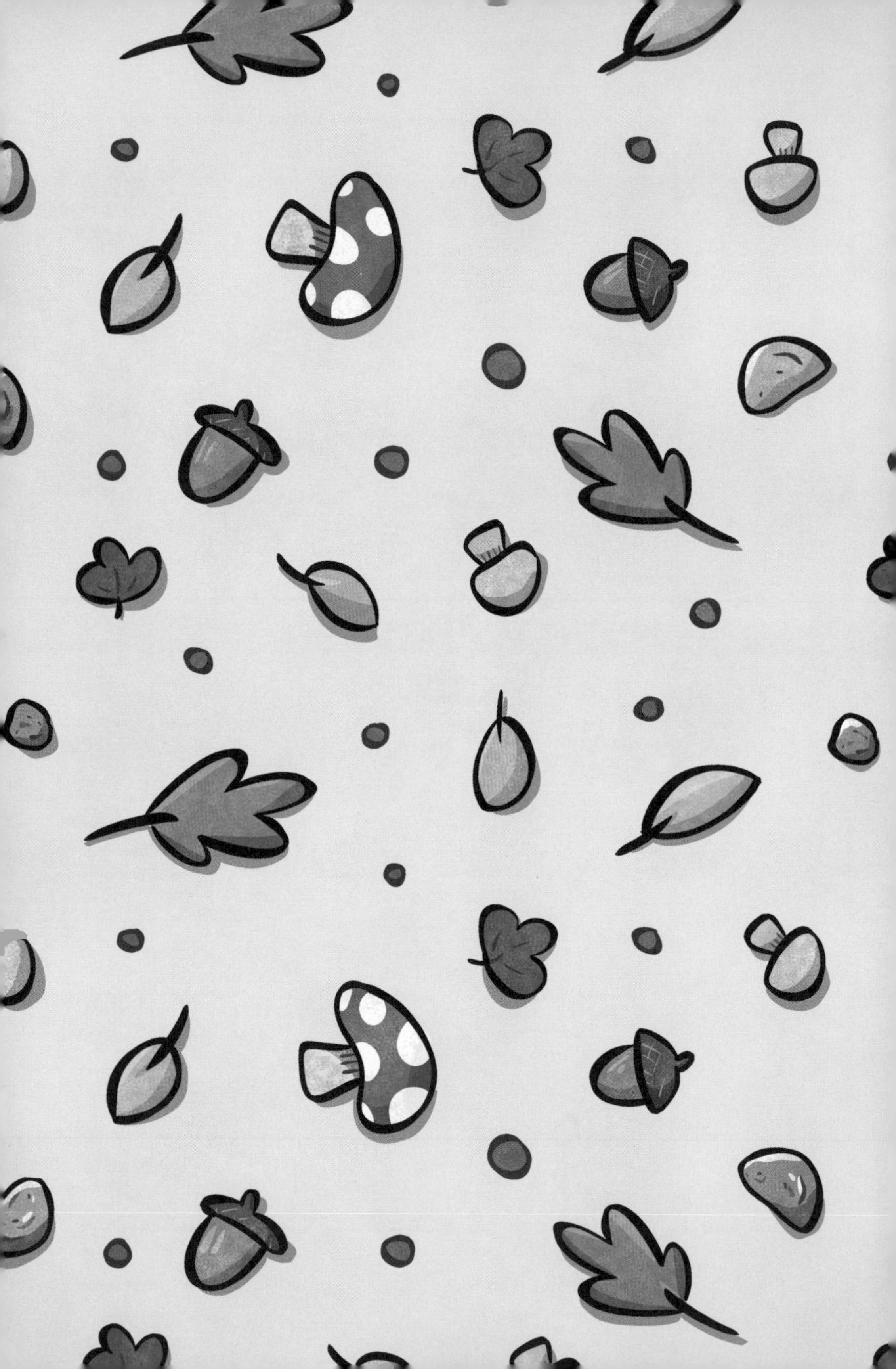

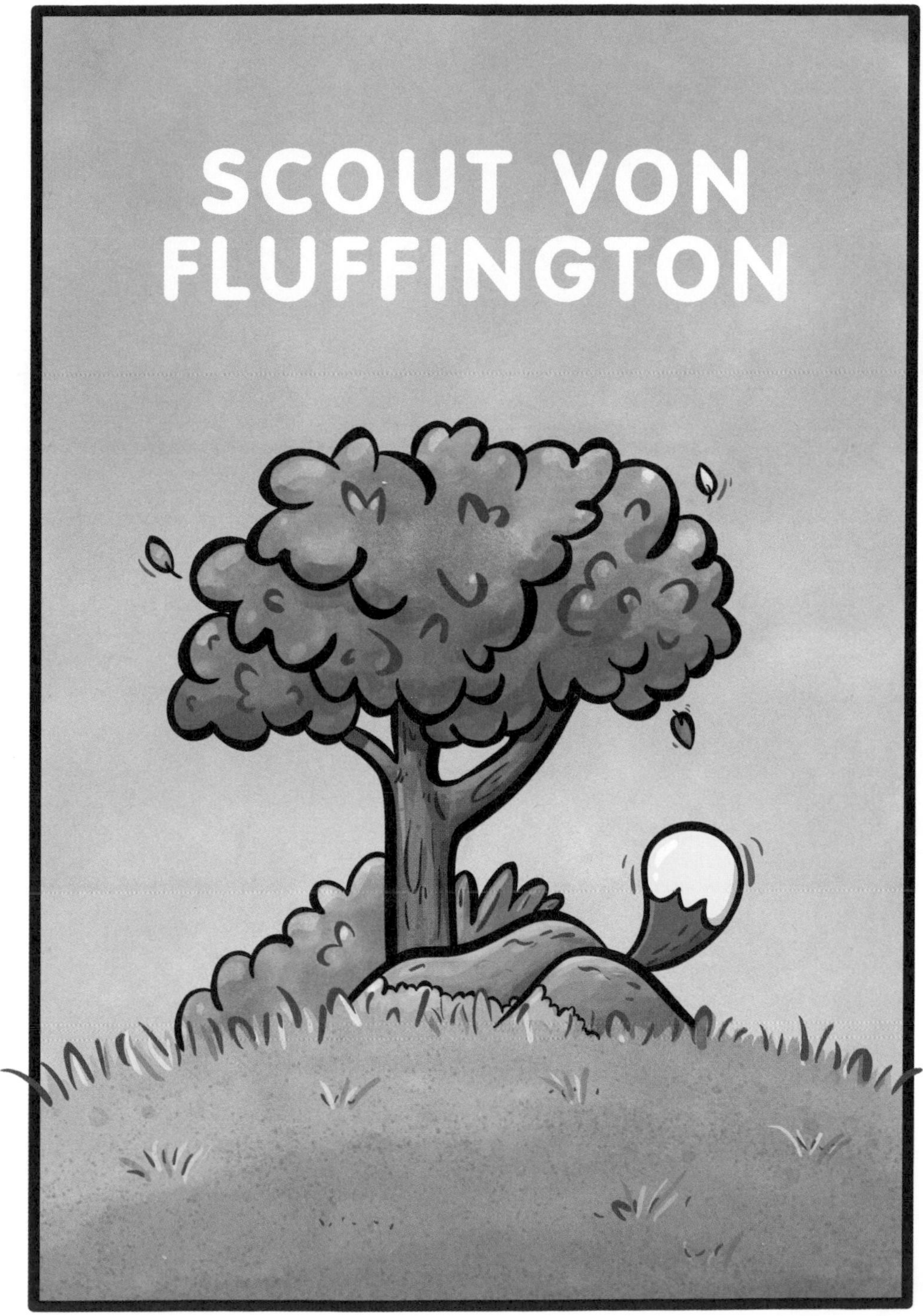
SCOUT VON
FLUFFINGTON

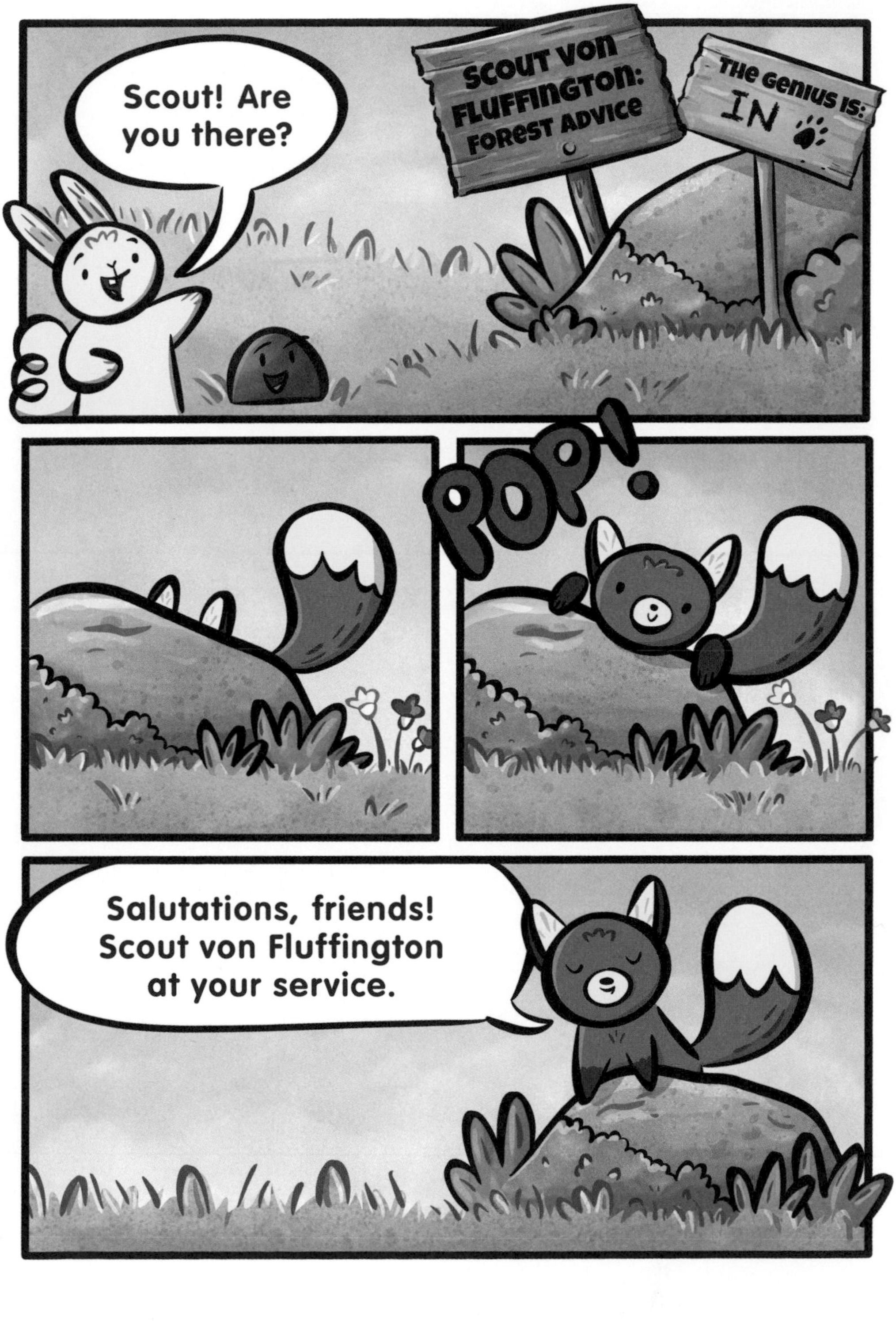
Scout! Are you there?
SCOUT VON FLUFFINGTON: FOREST ADVICE
THE GENIUS IS: IN
POP!
Salutations, friends! Scout von Fluffington at your service.

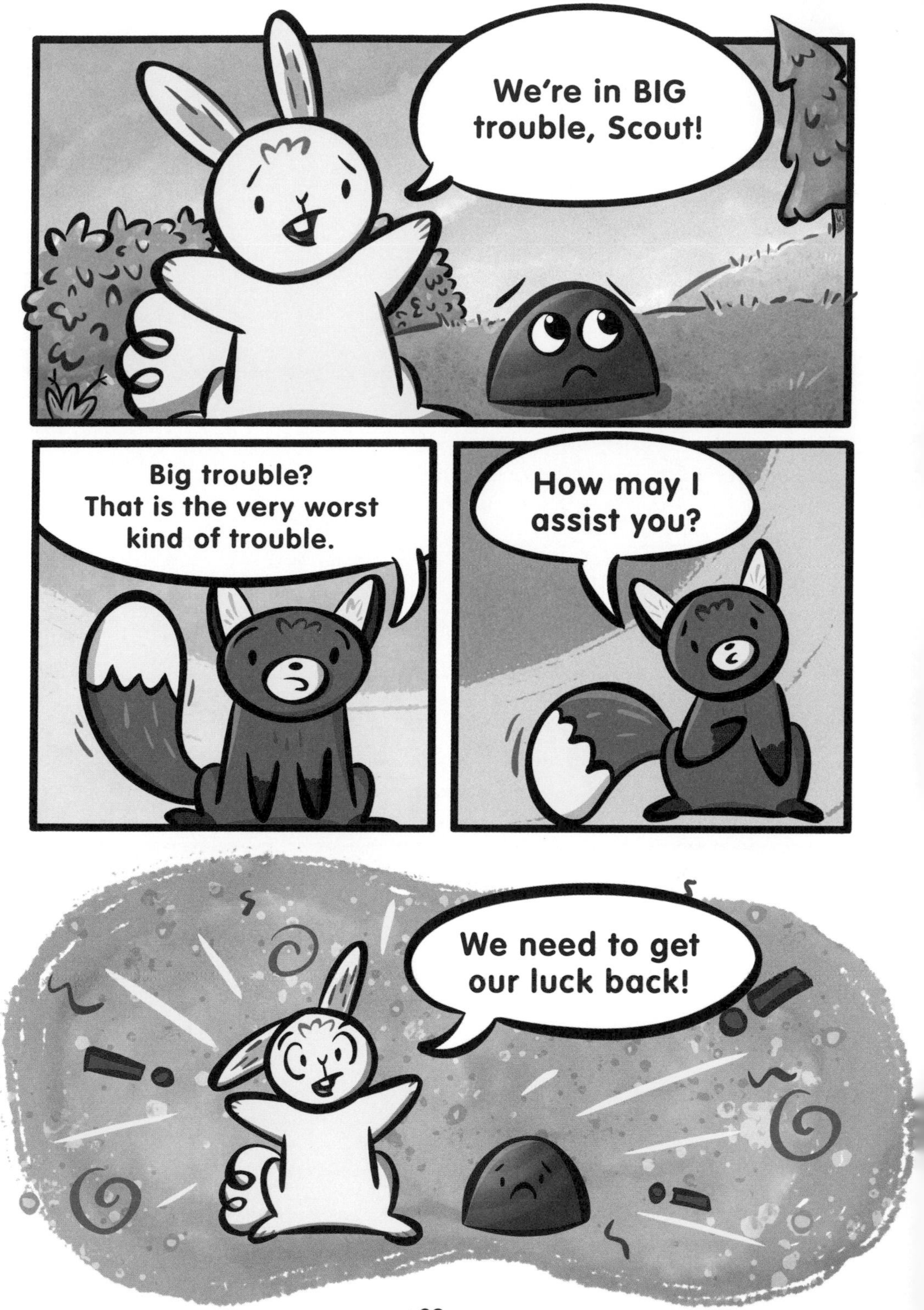
We're in BIG trouble, Scout!
Big trouble? That is the very worst kind of trouble.
How may I assist you?
We need to get our luck back!

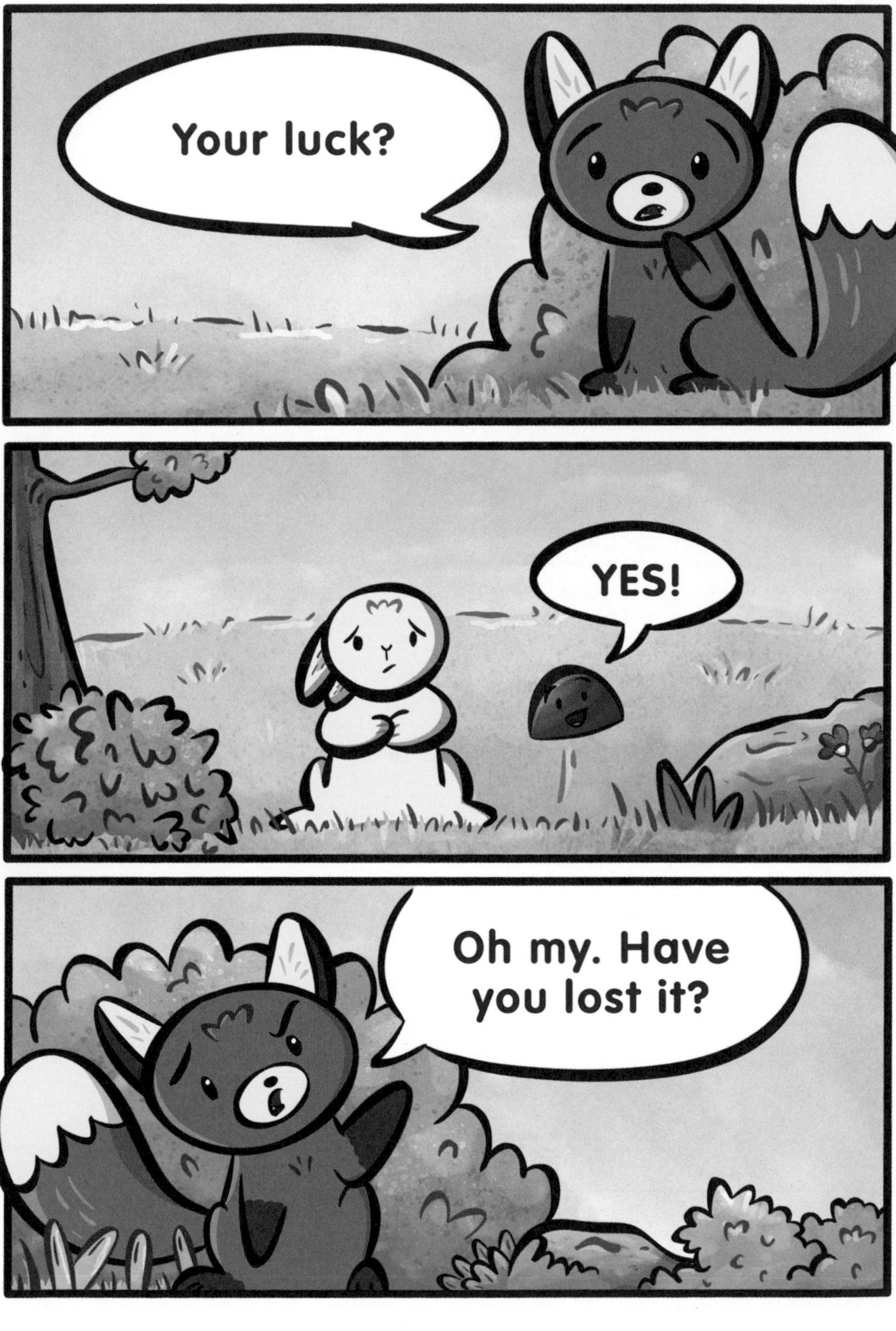
Your luck?
YES!
Oh my. Have you lost it?

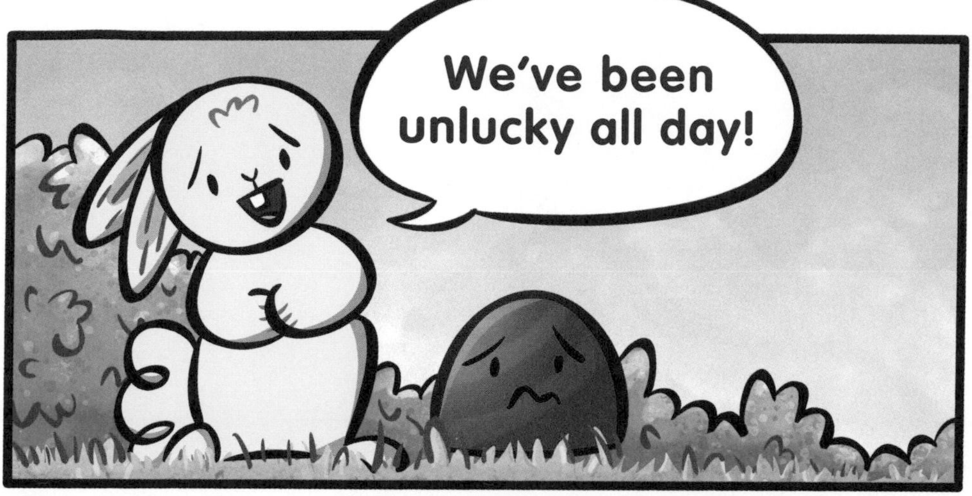
We've been unlucky all day!

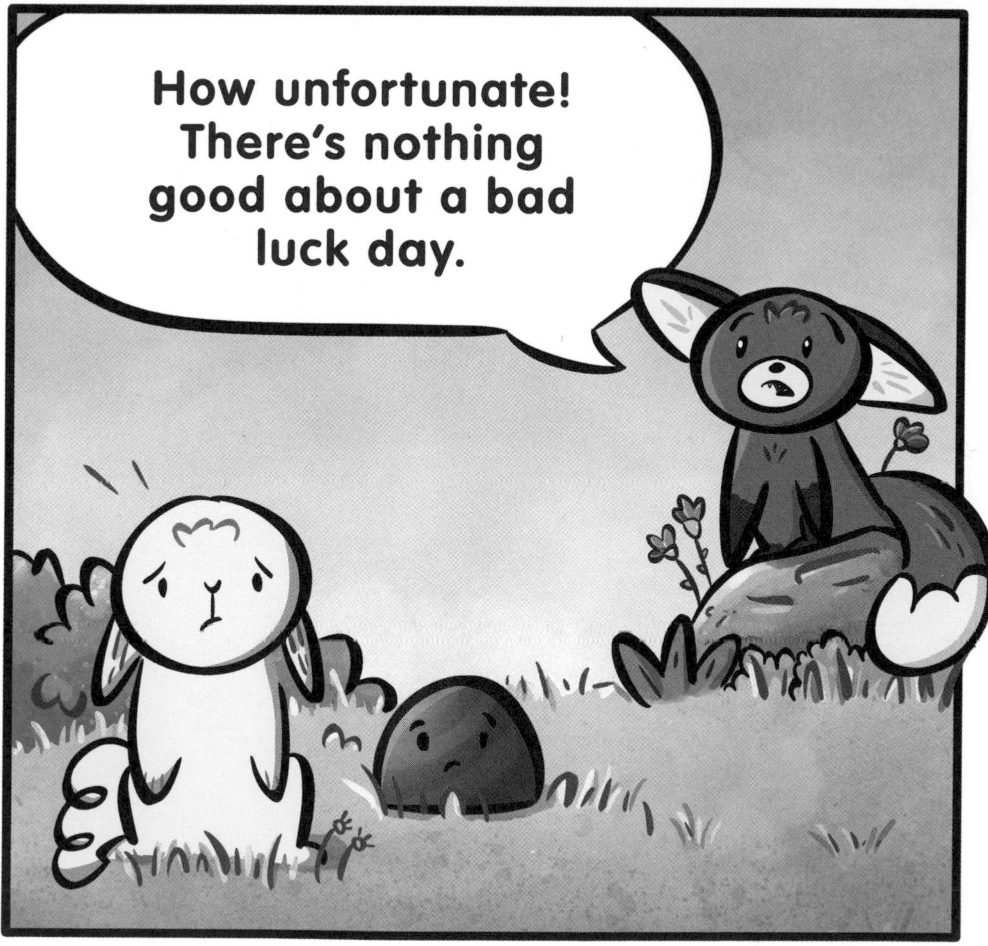
How unfortunate! There's nothing good about a bad luck day.

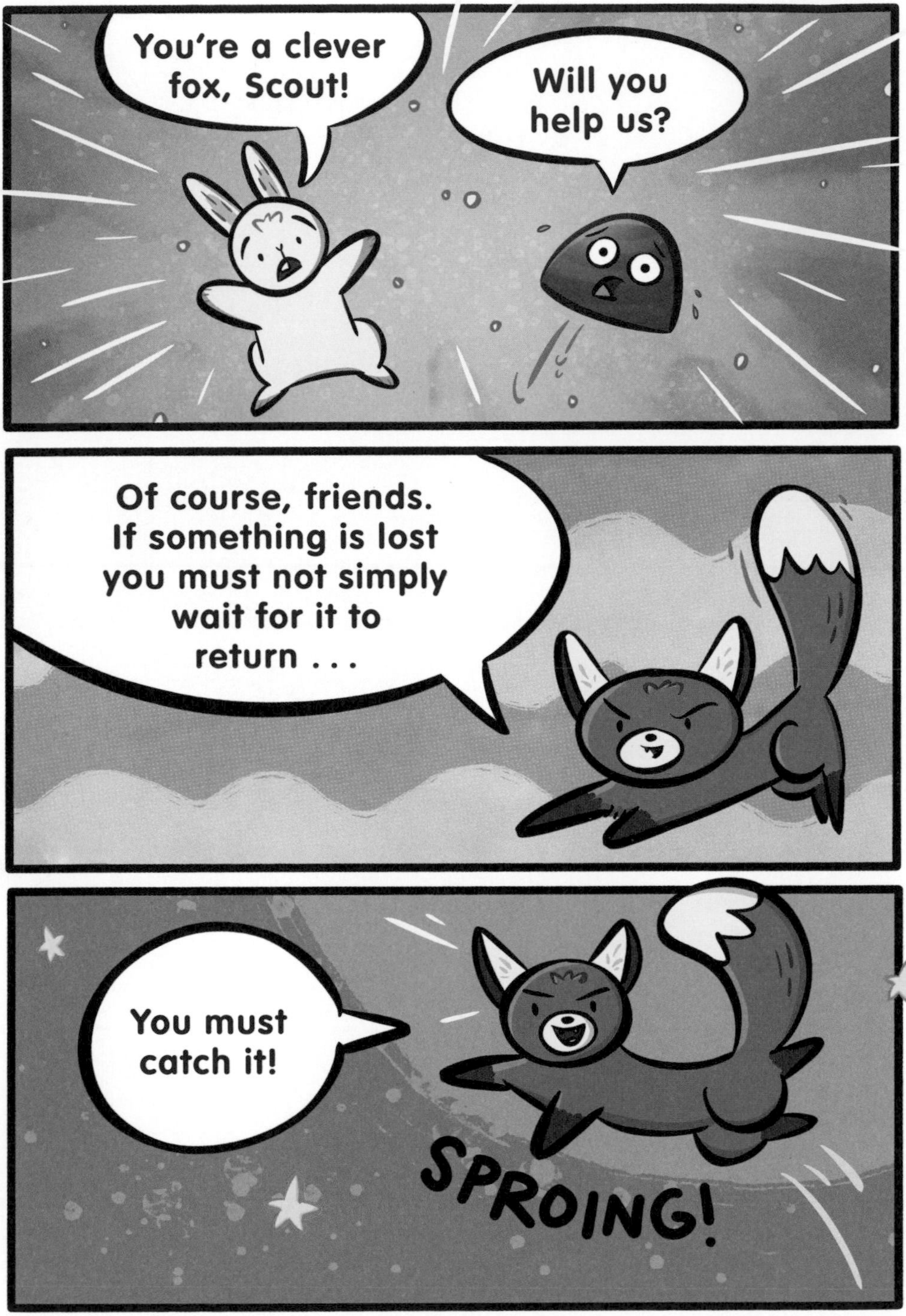
You're a clever fox, Scout!
Will you help us?
Of course, friends. If something is lost you must not simply wait for it to return . . .
You must catch it!
SPROING!

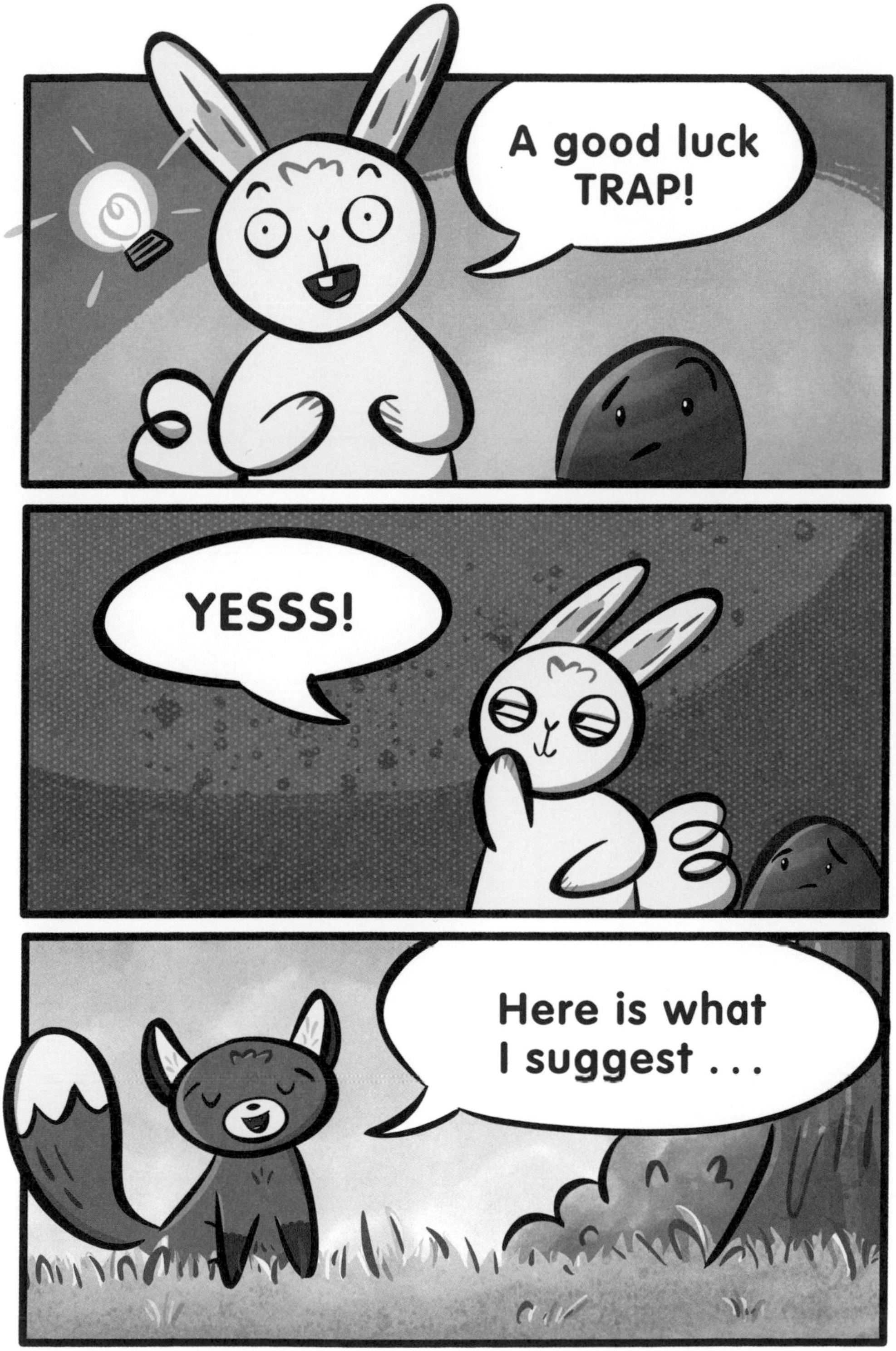
A good luck TRAP!
YESSS!
Here is what I suggest . . .

First, you must
set your trap . . .

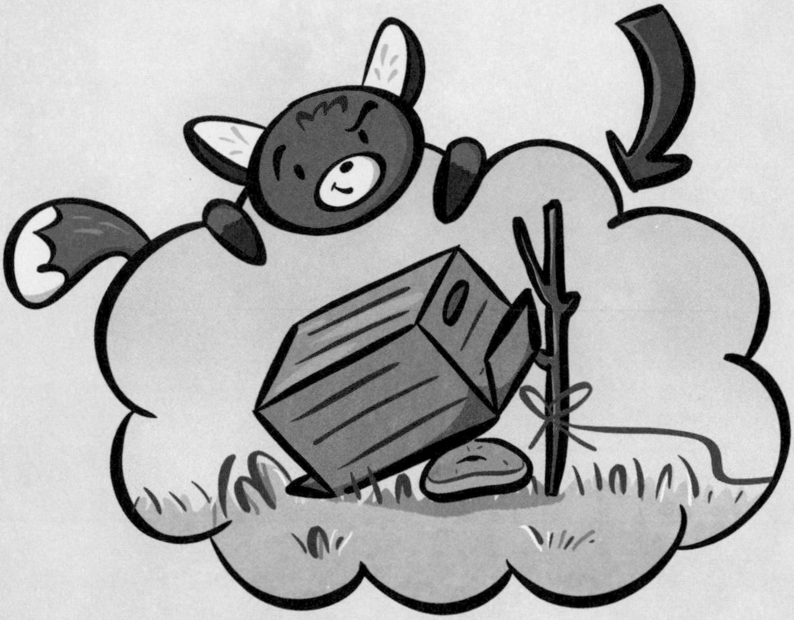

Use a delicious
treat as bait.

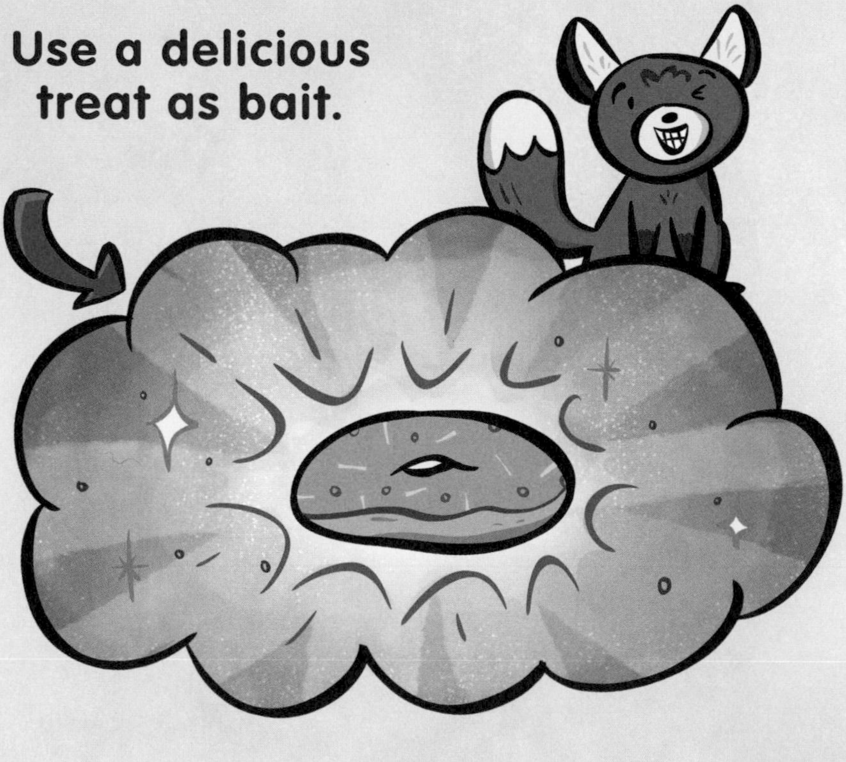

Wait until your luck comes along, and then . . .

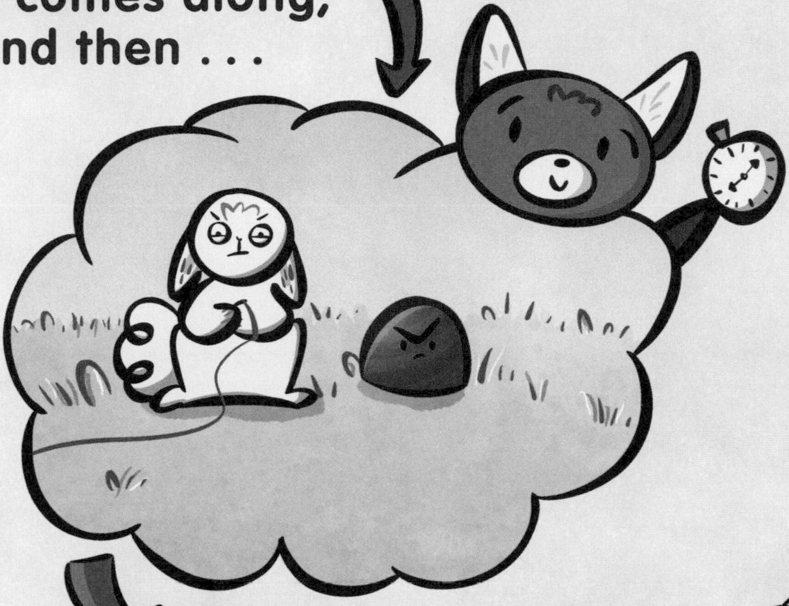

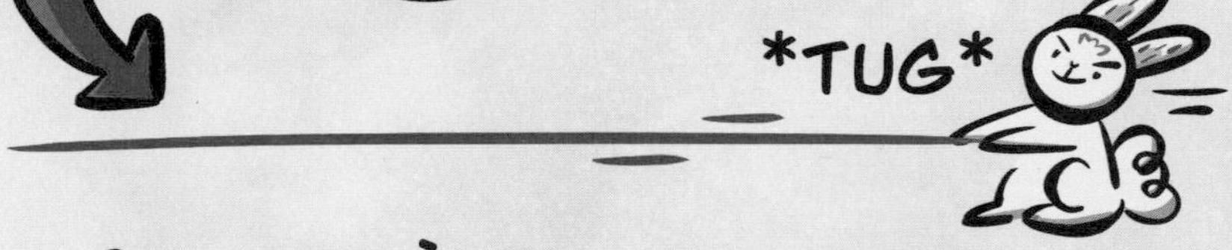
TUG

VOILÀ! You caught your luck!

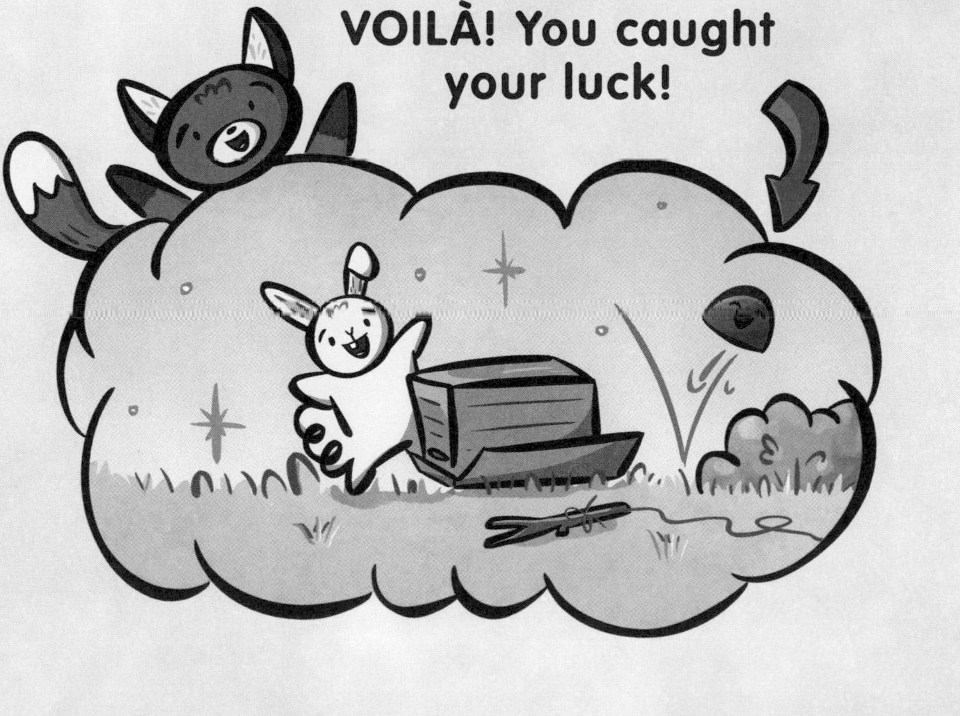

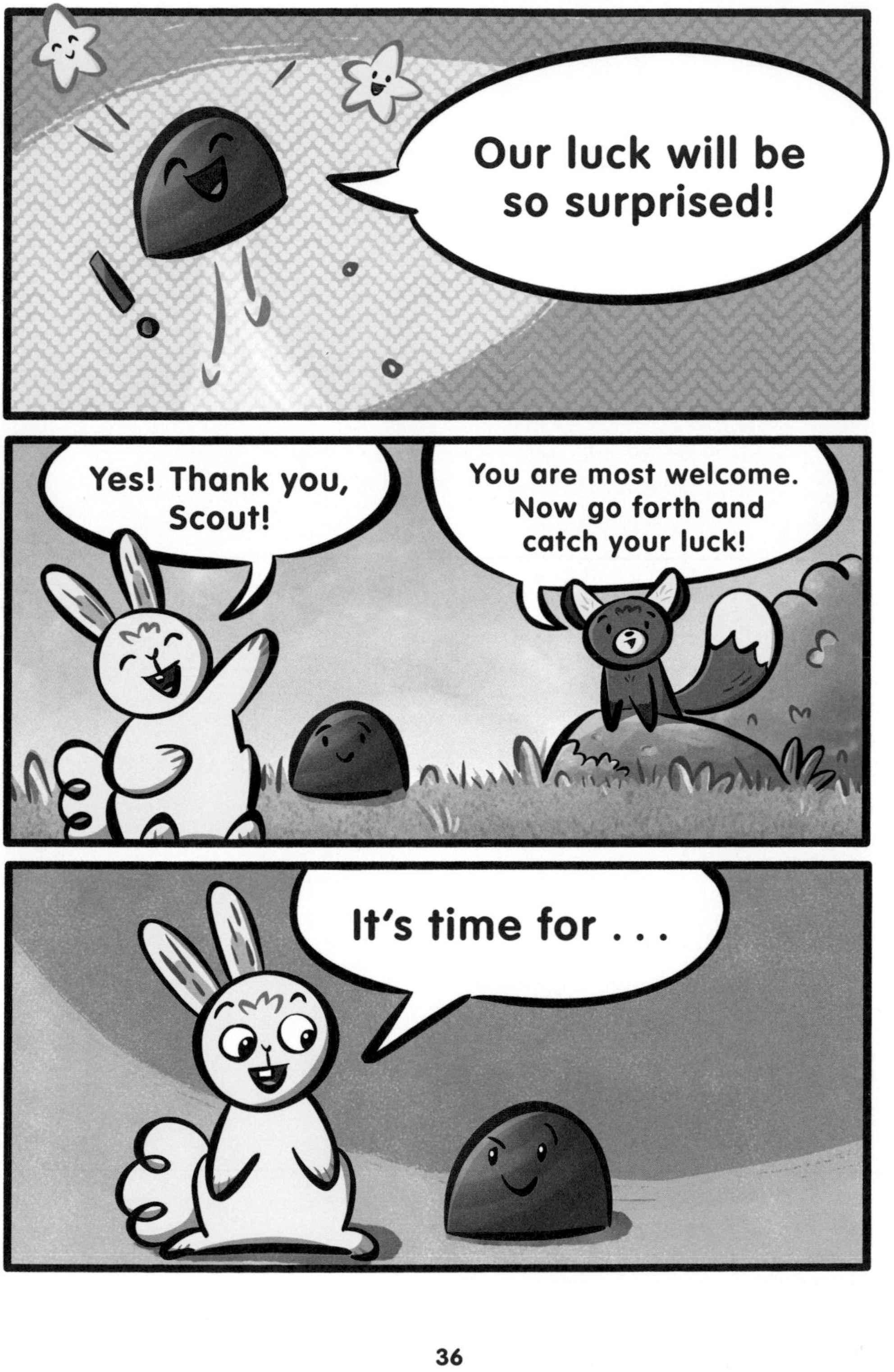
Our luck will be so surprised!
Yes! Thank you, Scout!
You are most welcome. Now go forth and catch your luck!
It's time for . . .

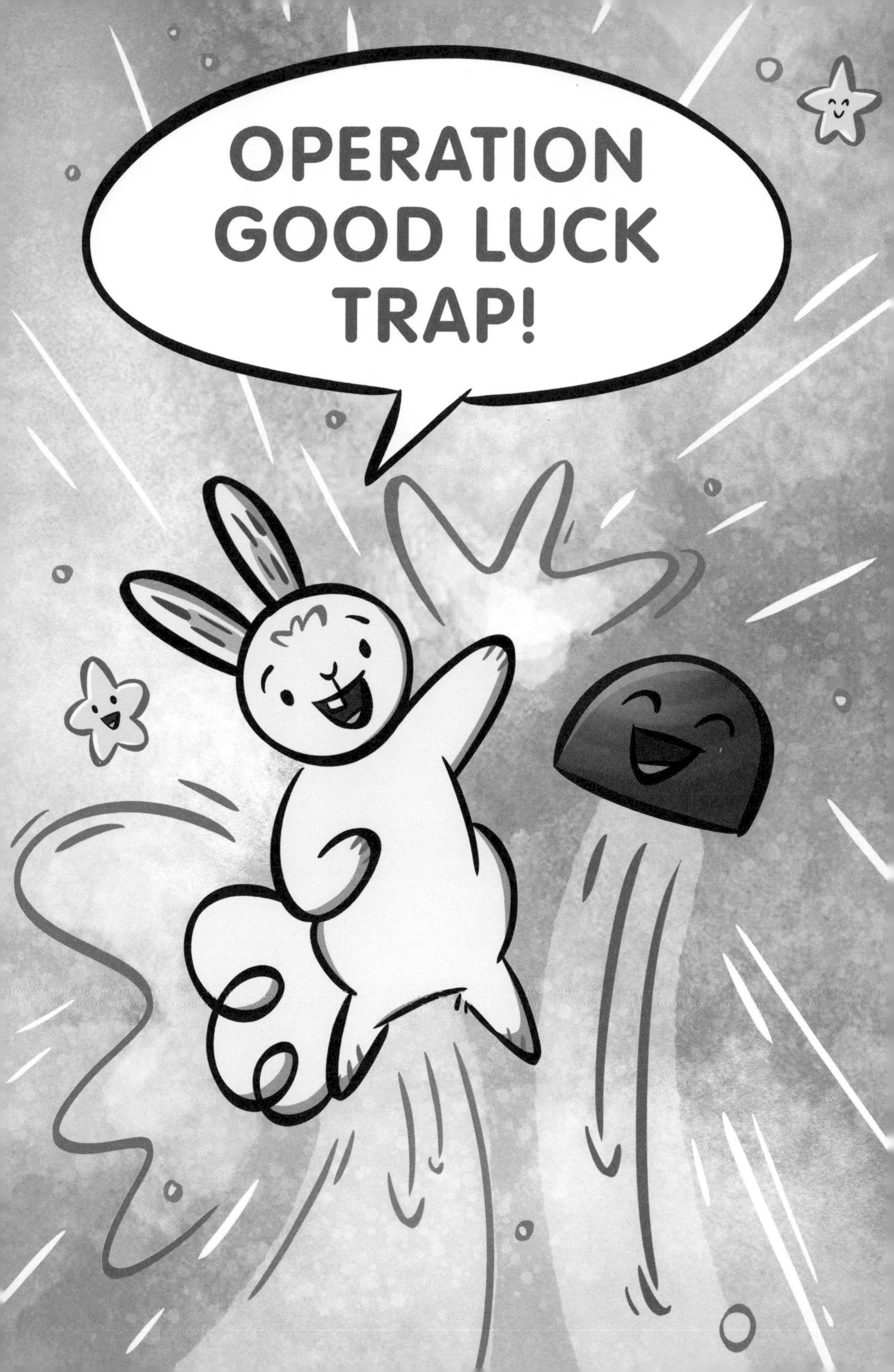
OPERATION GOOD LUCK TRAP!

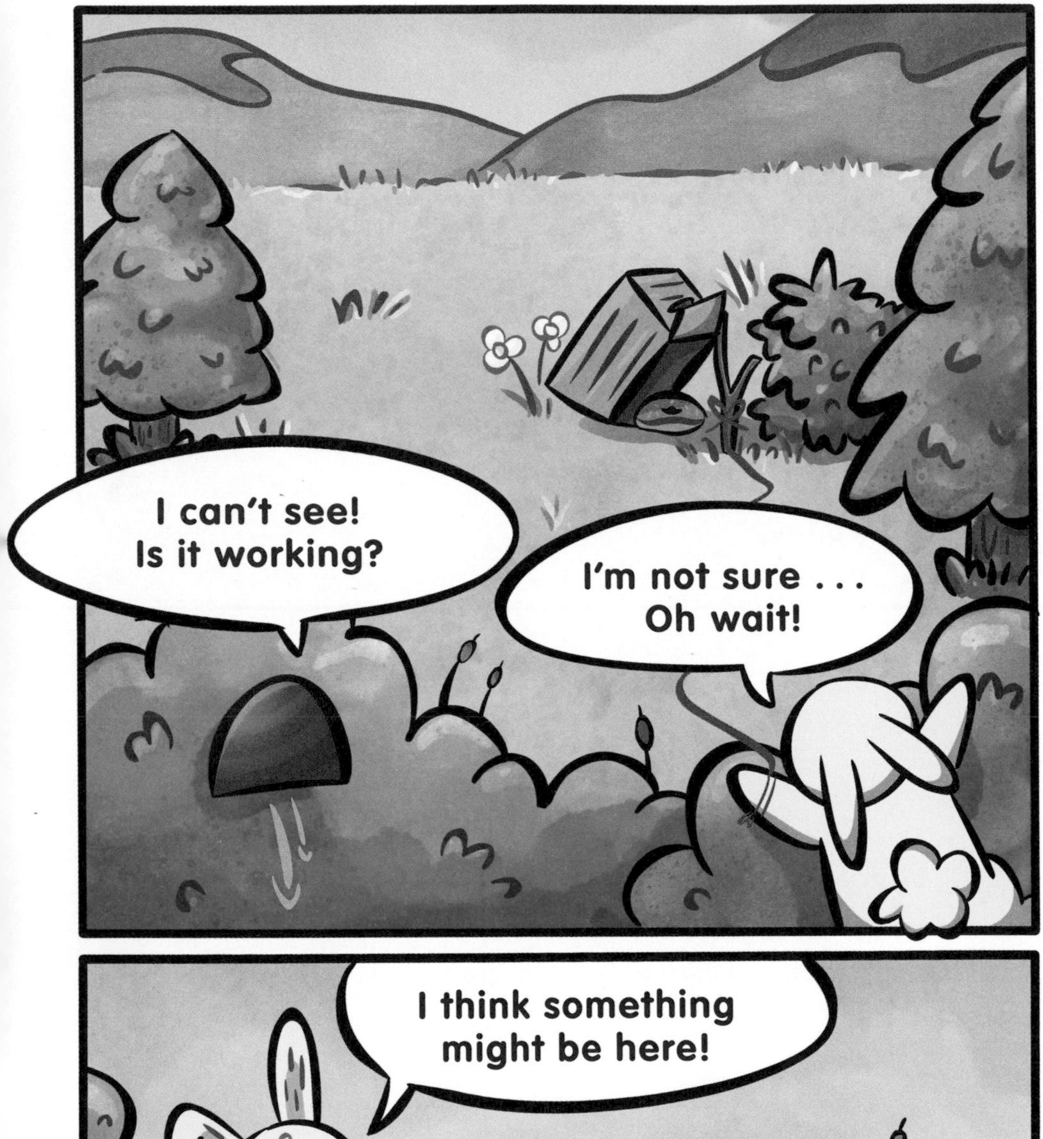
I can't see!
Is it working?
I'm not sure . . .
Oh wait!

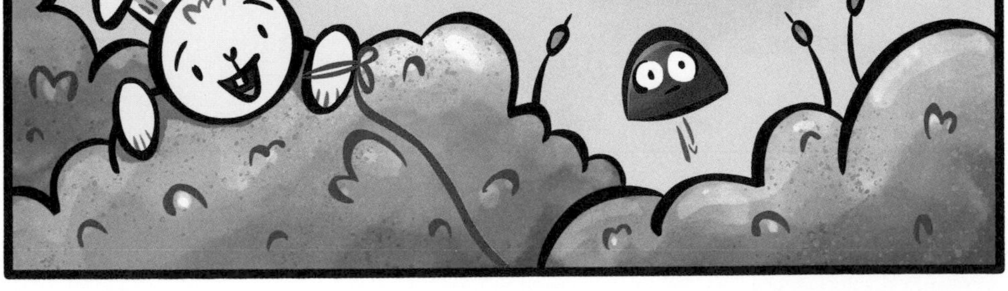
I think something
might be here!

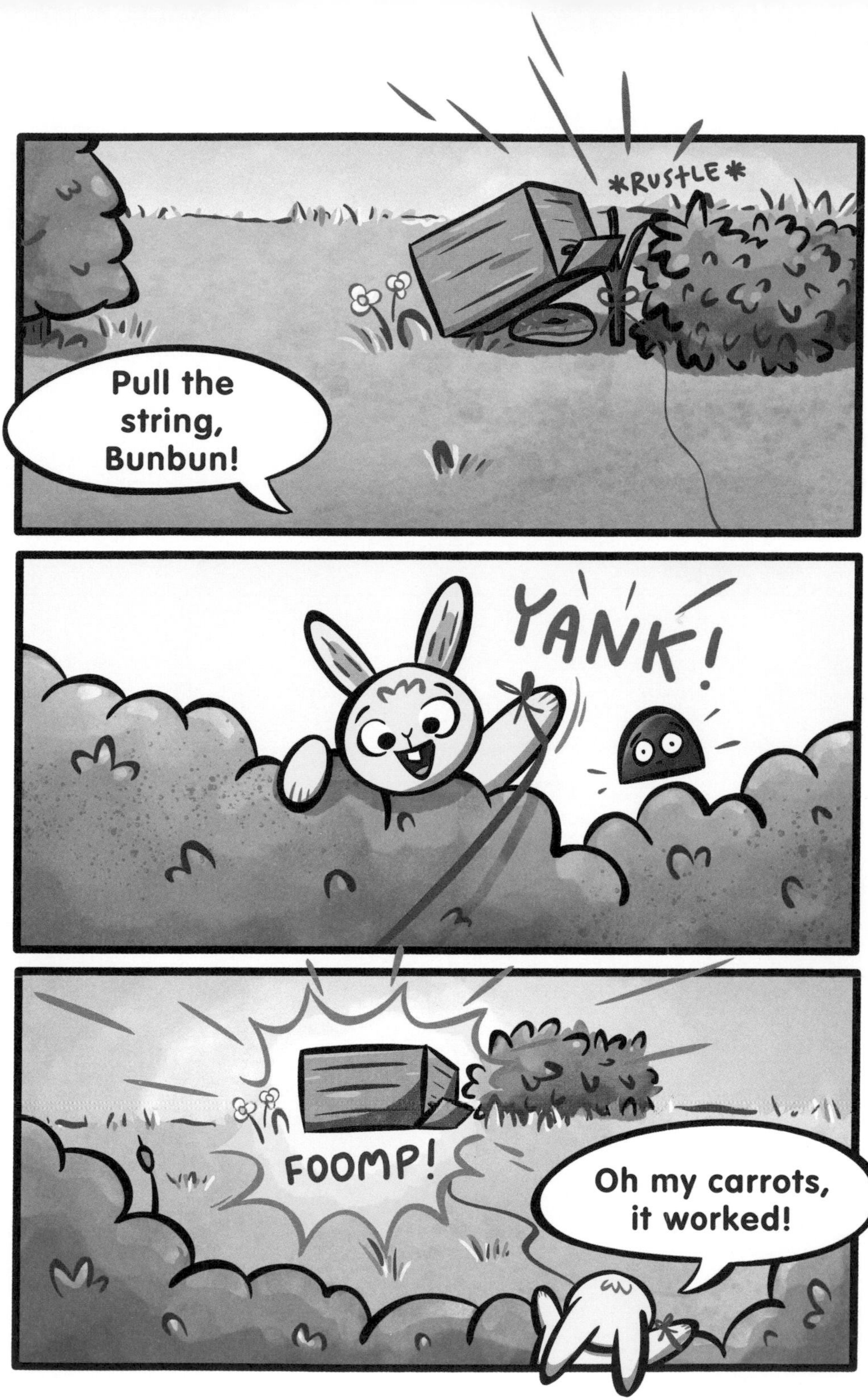
RUSTLE
Pull the string, Bunbun!
YANK!
FOOMP!
Oh my carrots, it worked!

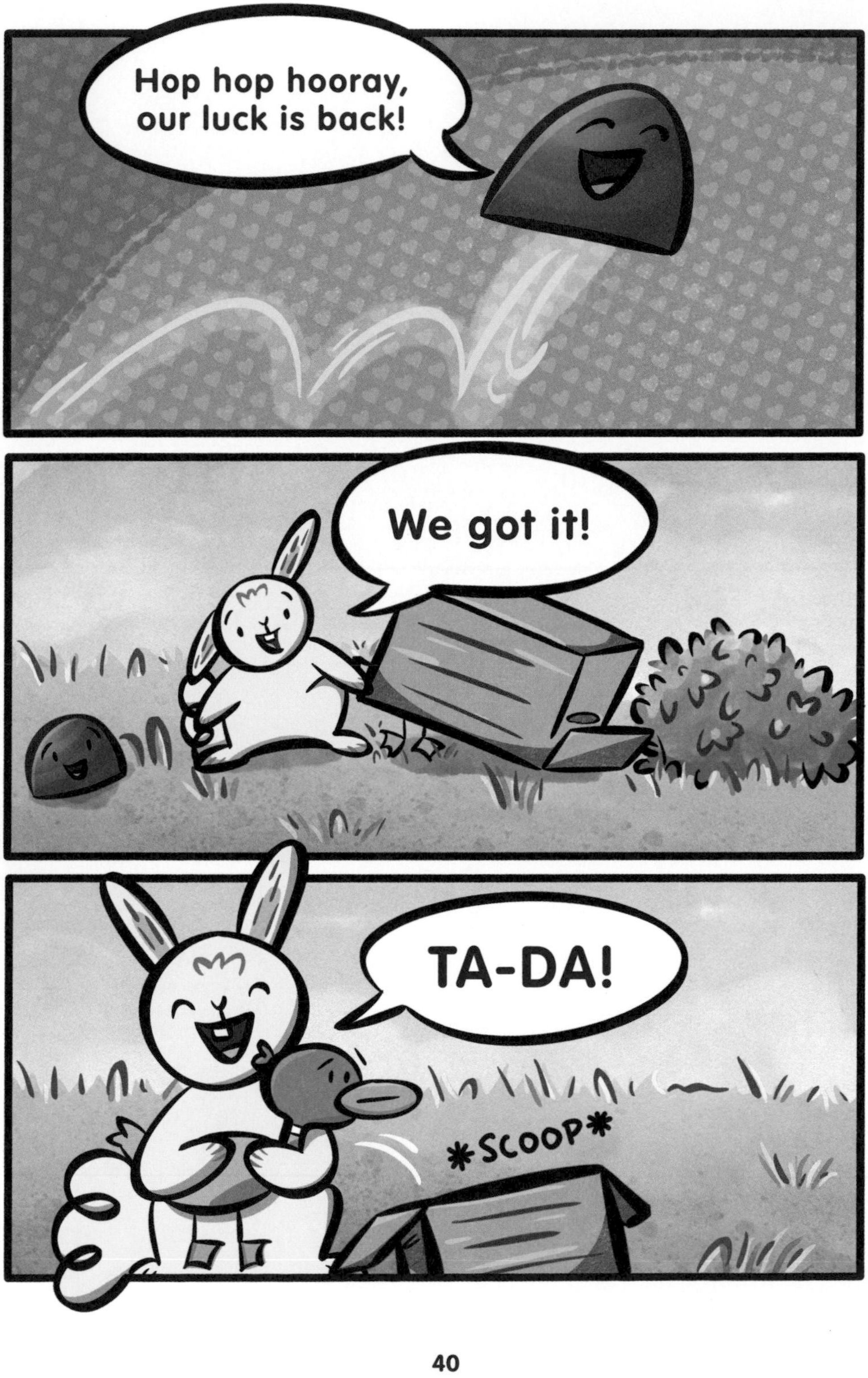
Hop hop hooray, our luck is back!
We got it!
TA-DA!
SCOOP

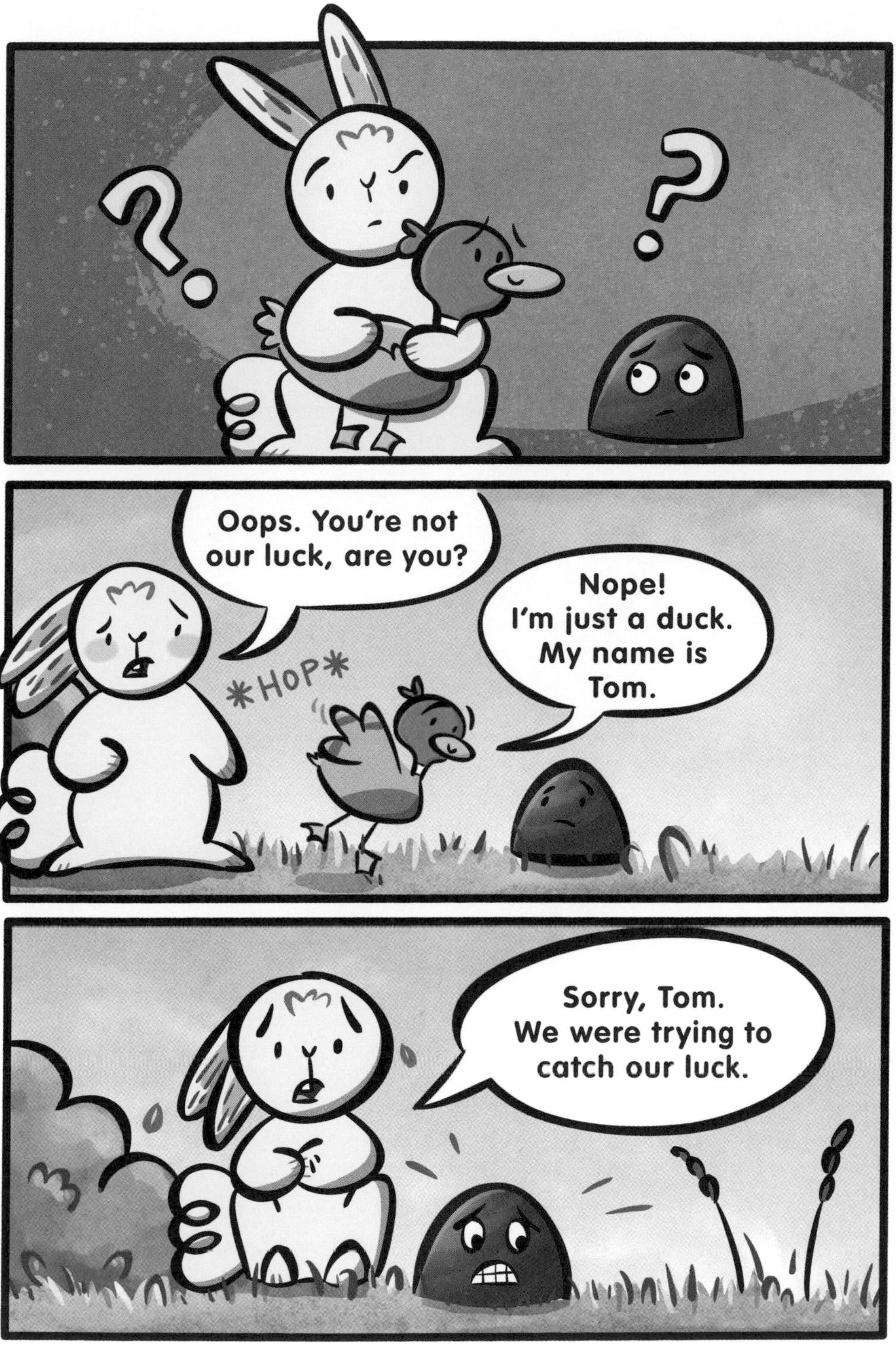
Oops. You're not our luck, are you?
HOP
Nope! I'm just a duck. My name is Tom.
Sorry, Tom. We were trying to catch our luck.

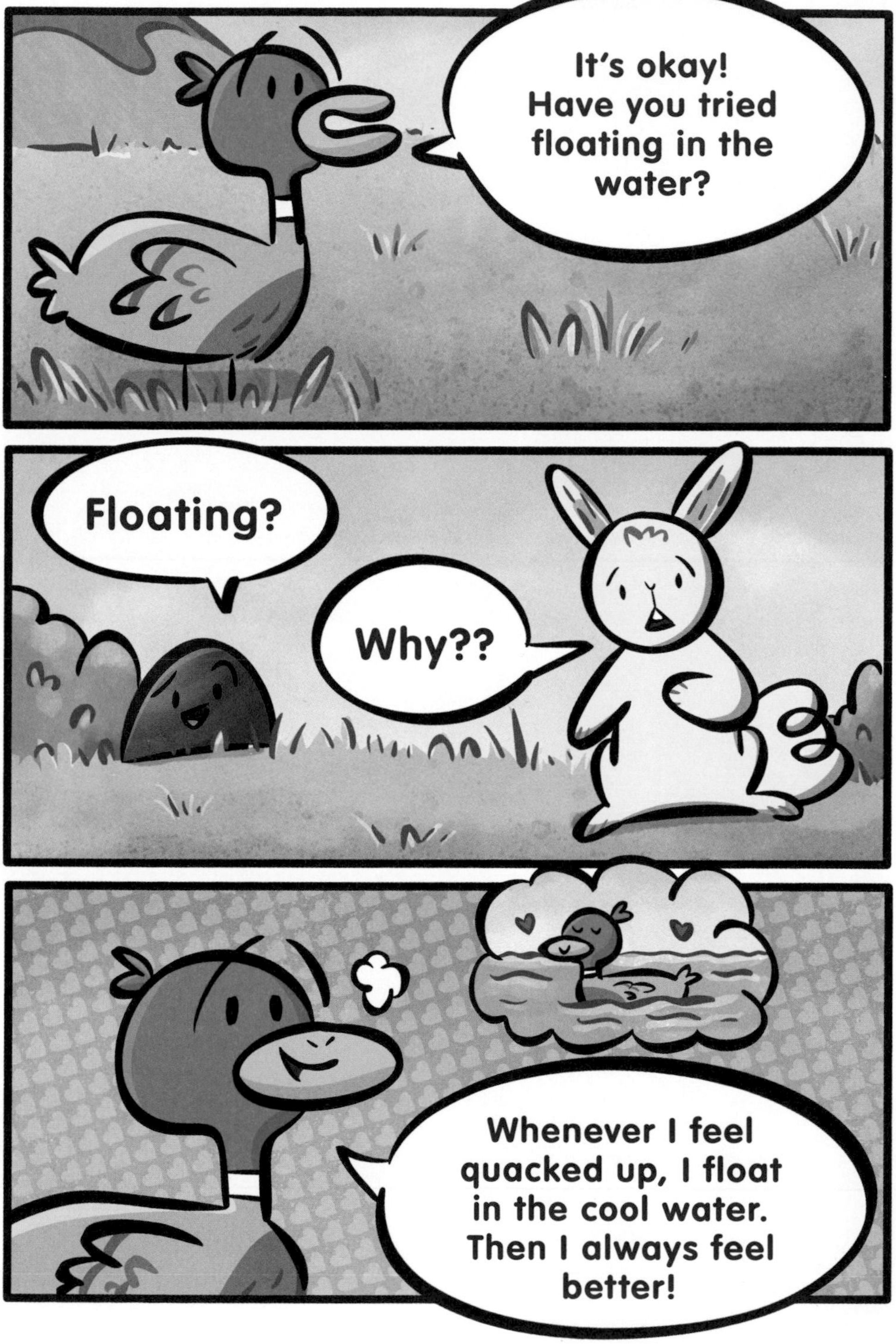
It's okay!
Have you tried
floating in the
water?
Floating?
Why??
Whenever I feel
quacked up, I float
in the cool water.
Then I always feel
better!

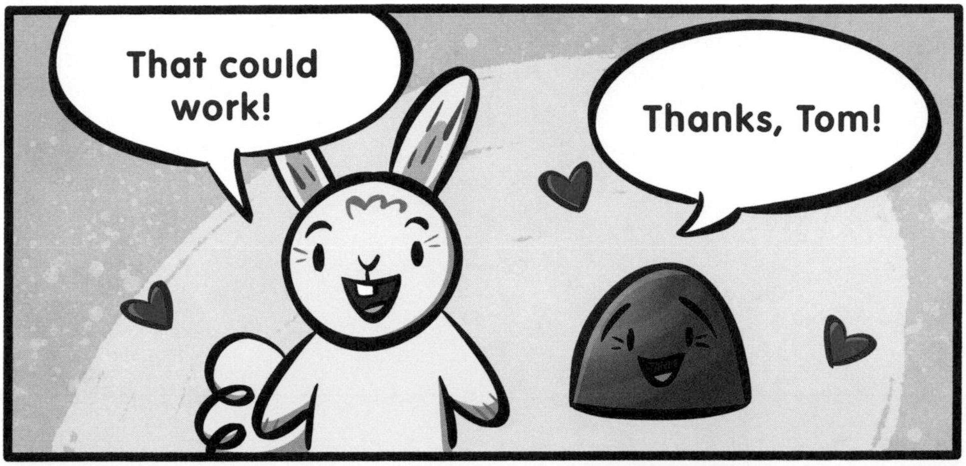
That could work!
Thanks, Tom!

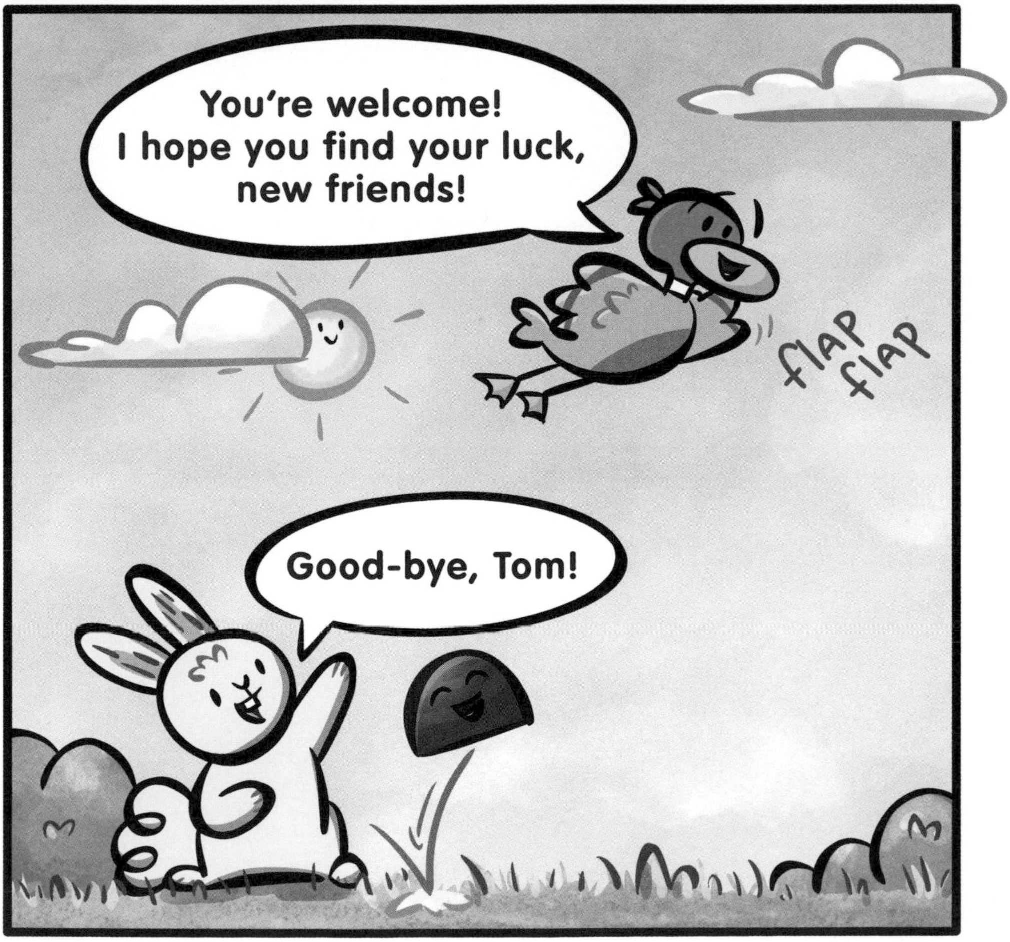
You're welcome! I hope you find your luck, new friends!
flap flap
Good-bye, Tom!

AND SO . . .

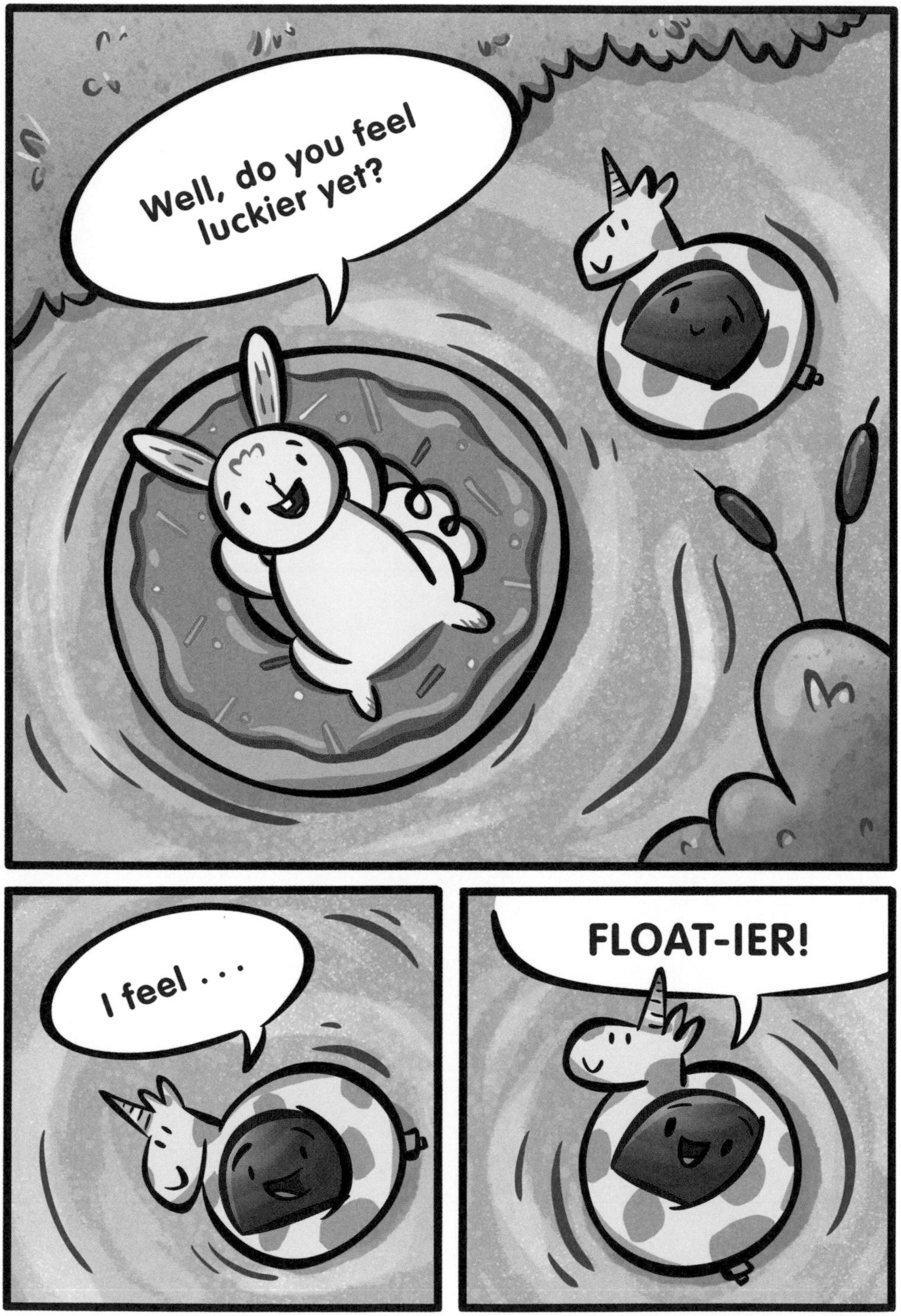
Well, do you feel luckier yet?
I feel . . .
FLOAT-IER!

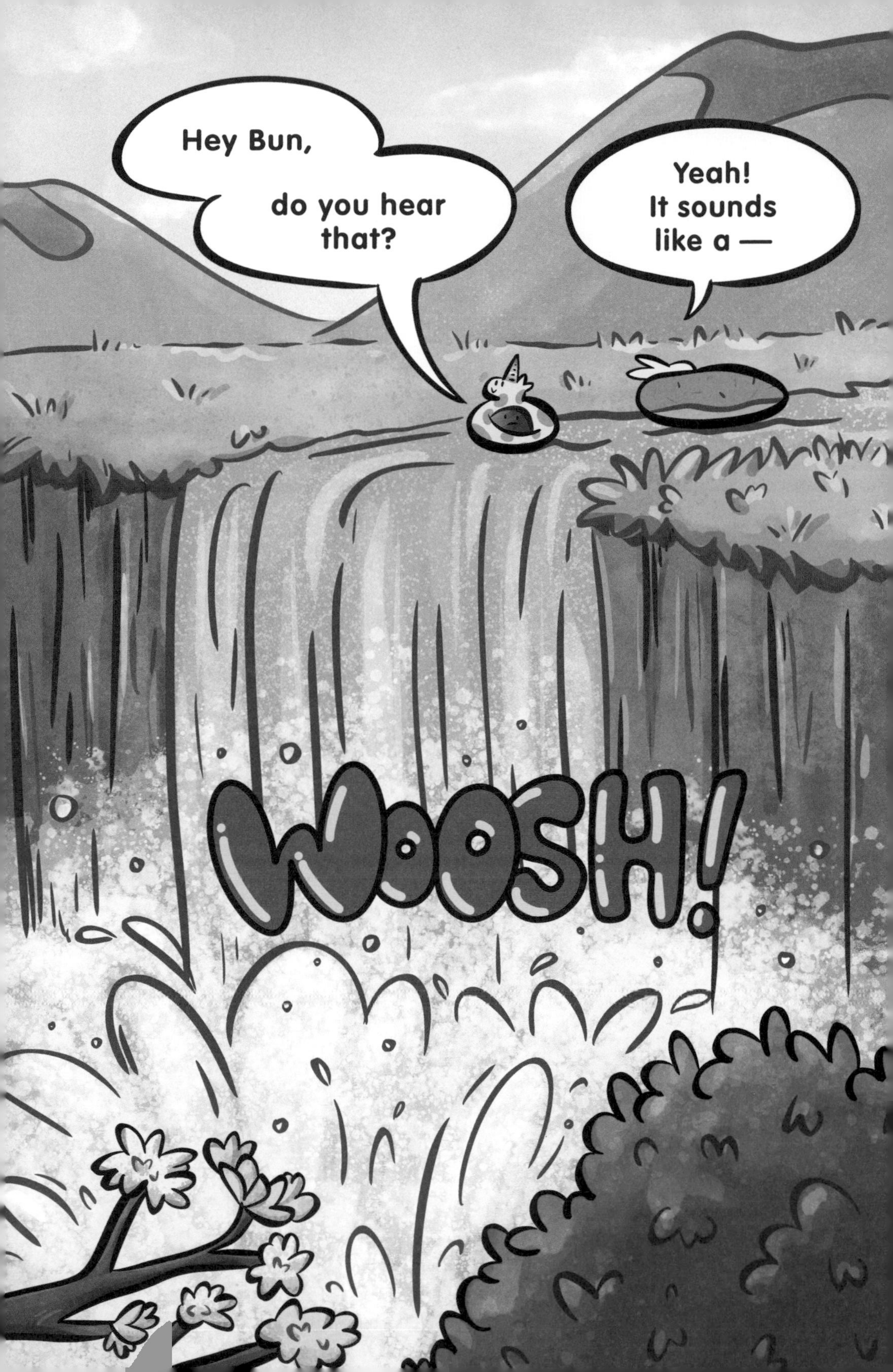
Hey Bun,
do you hear that?
Yeah! It sounds like a —
WOOSH!

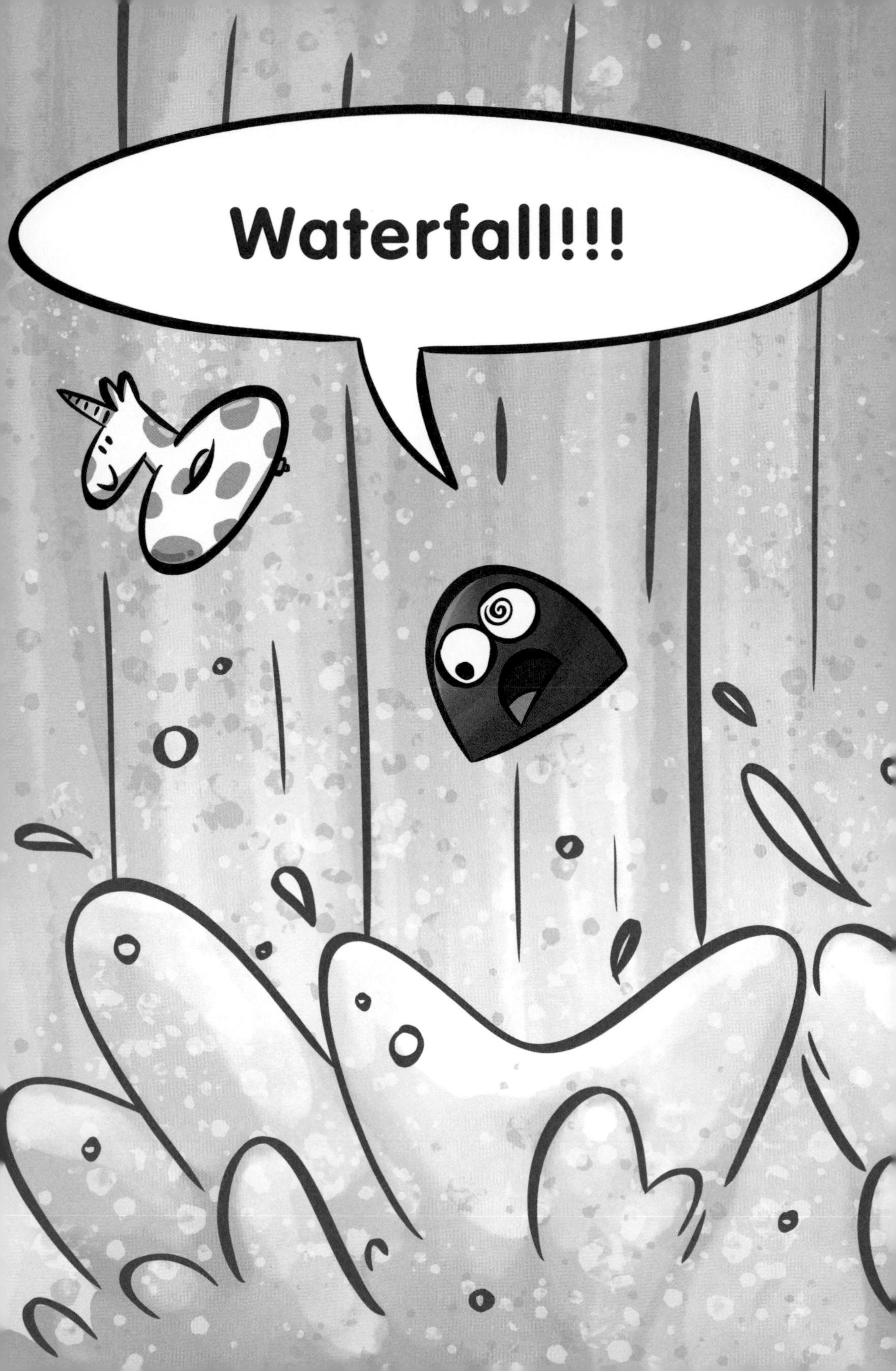
Waterfall!!!

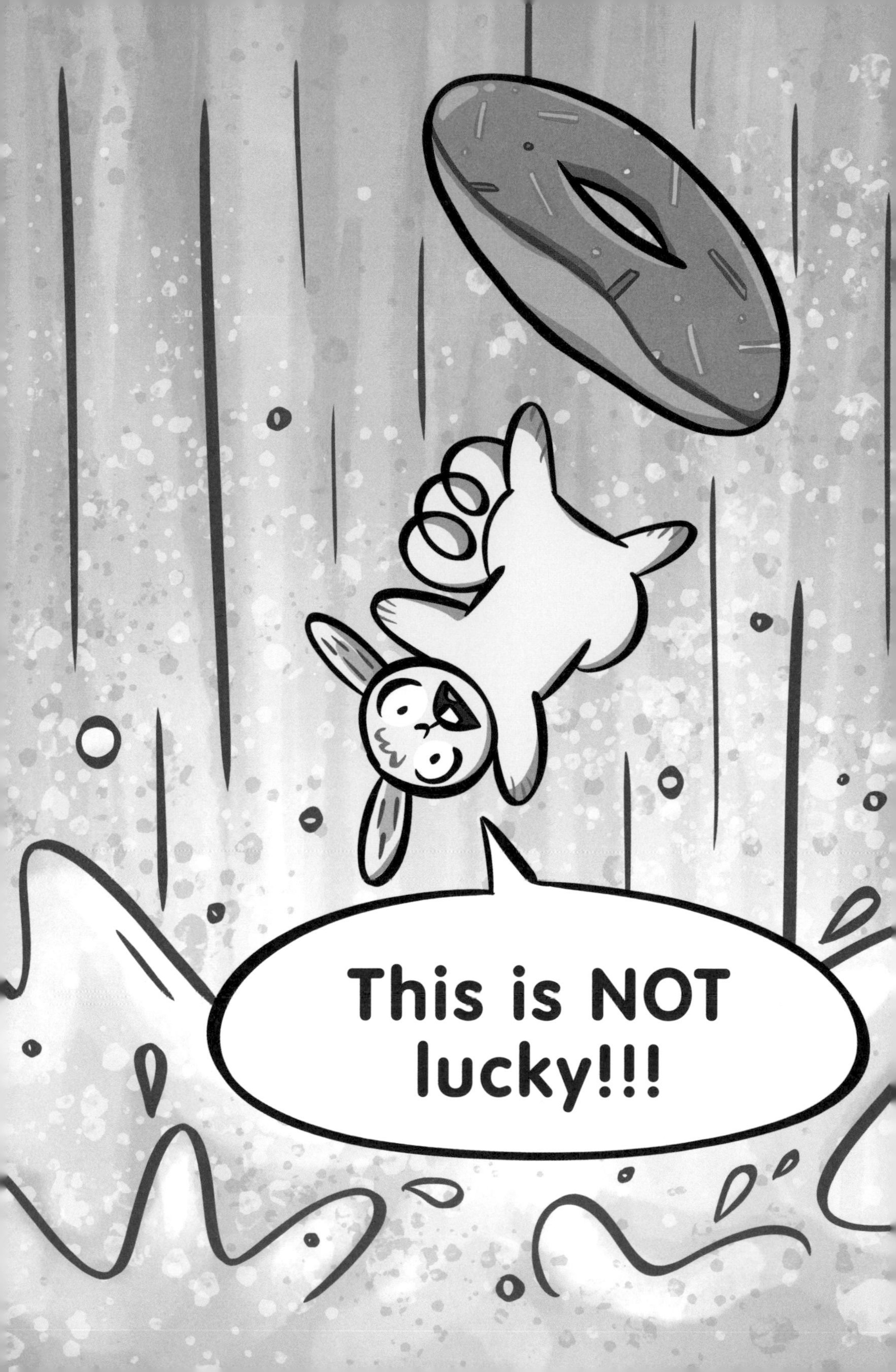
This is NOT lucky!!!

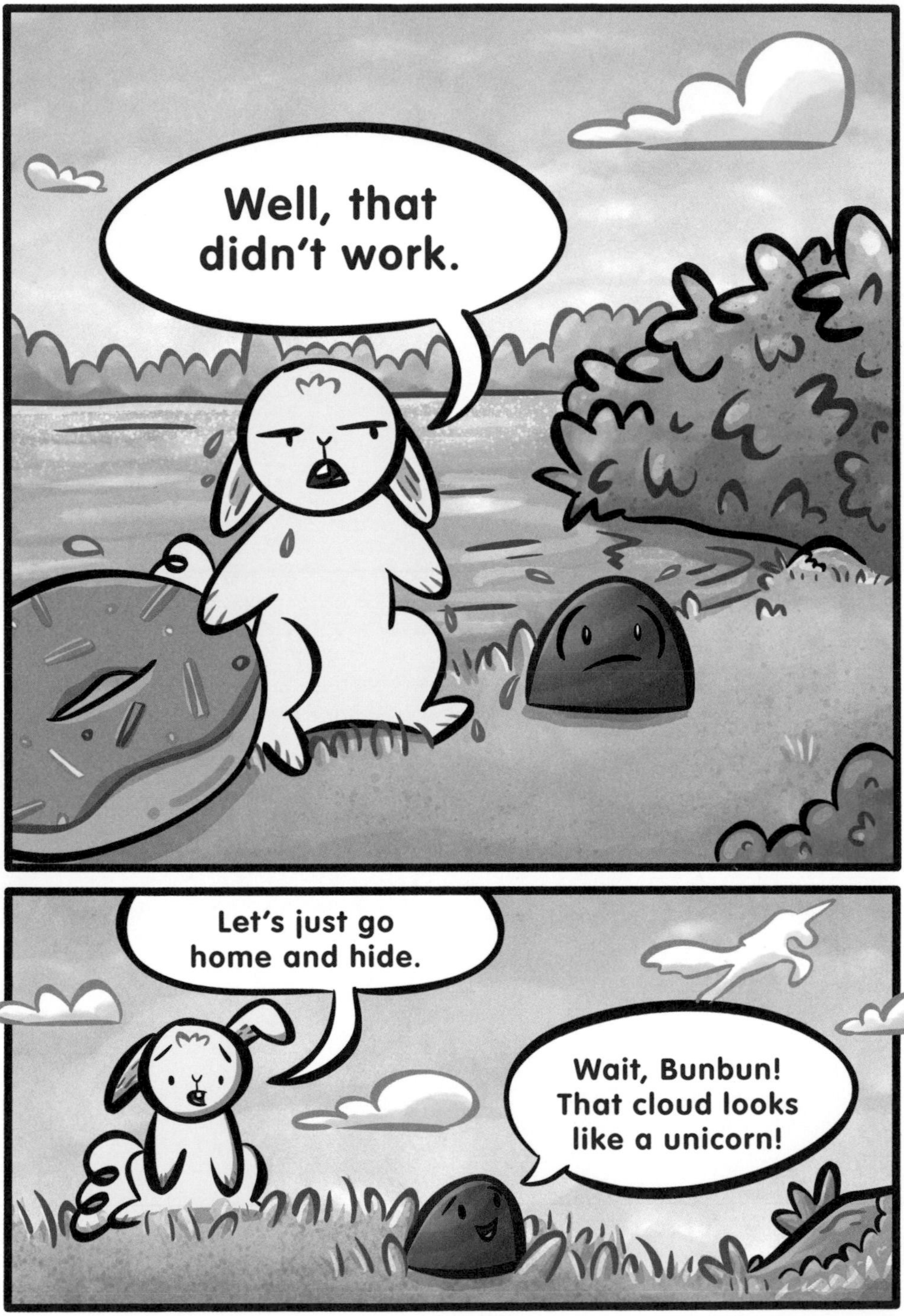
Well, that didn't work.
Let's just go home and hide.
Wait, Bunbun! That cloud looks like a unicorn!

DID SOMEONE SAY UNICORN?

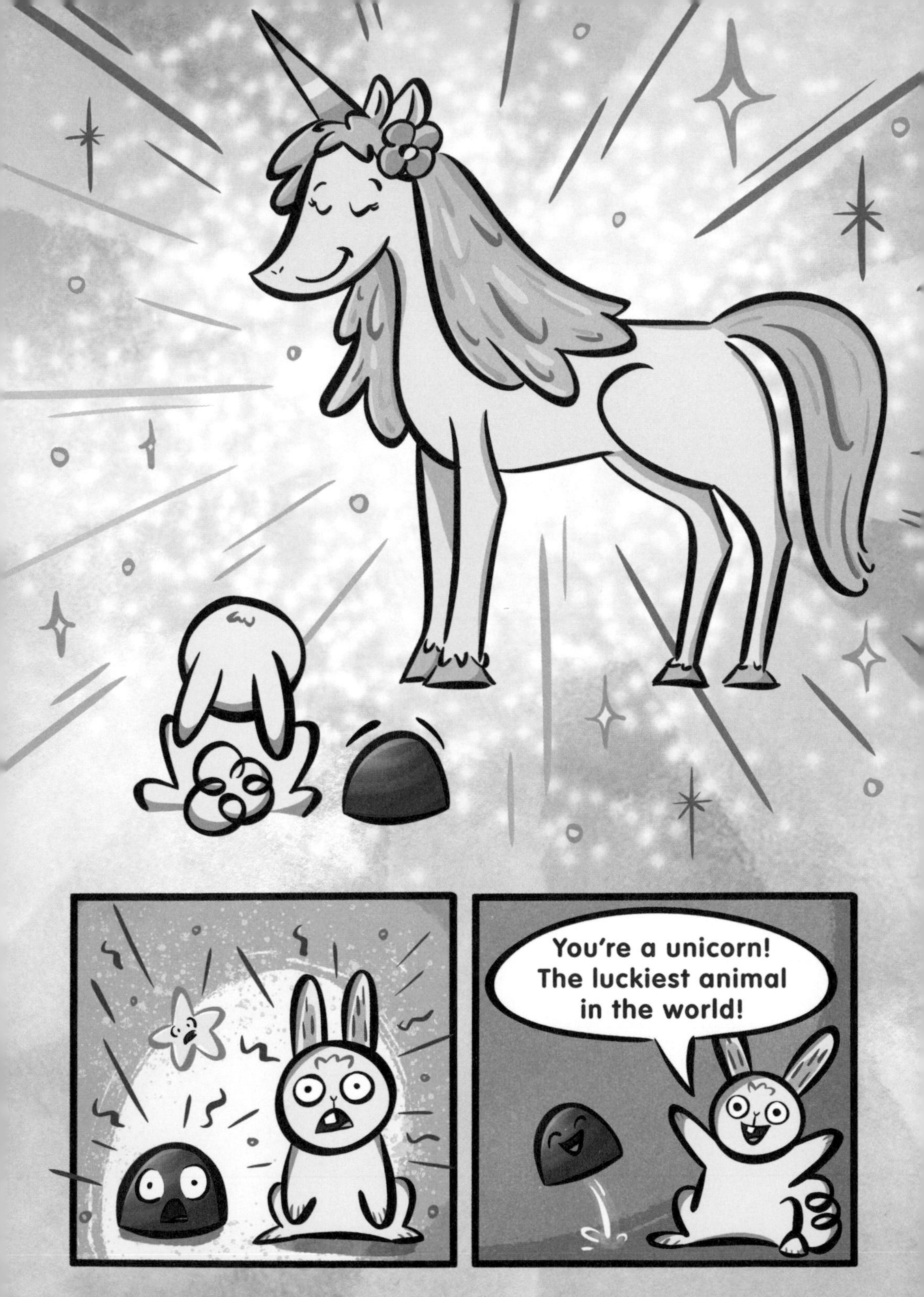
You're a unicorn!
The luckiest animal
in the world!

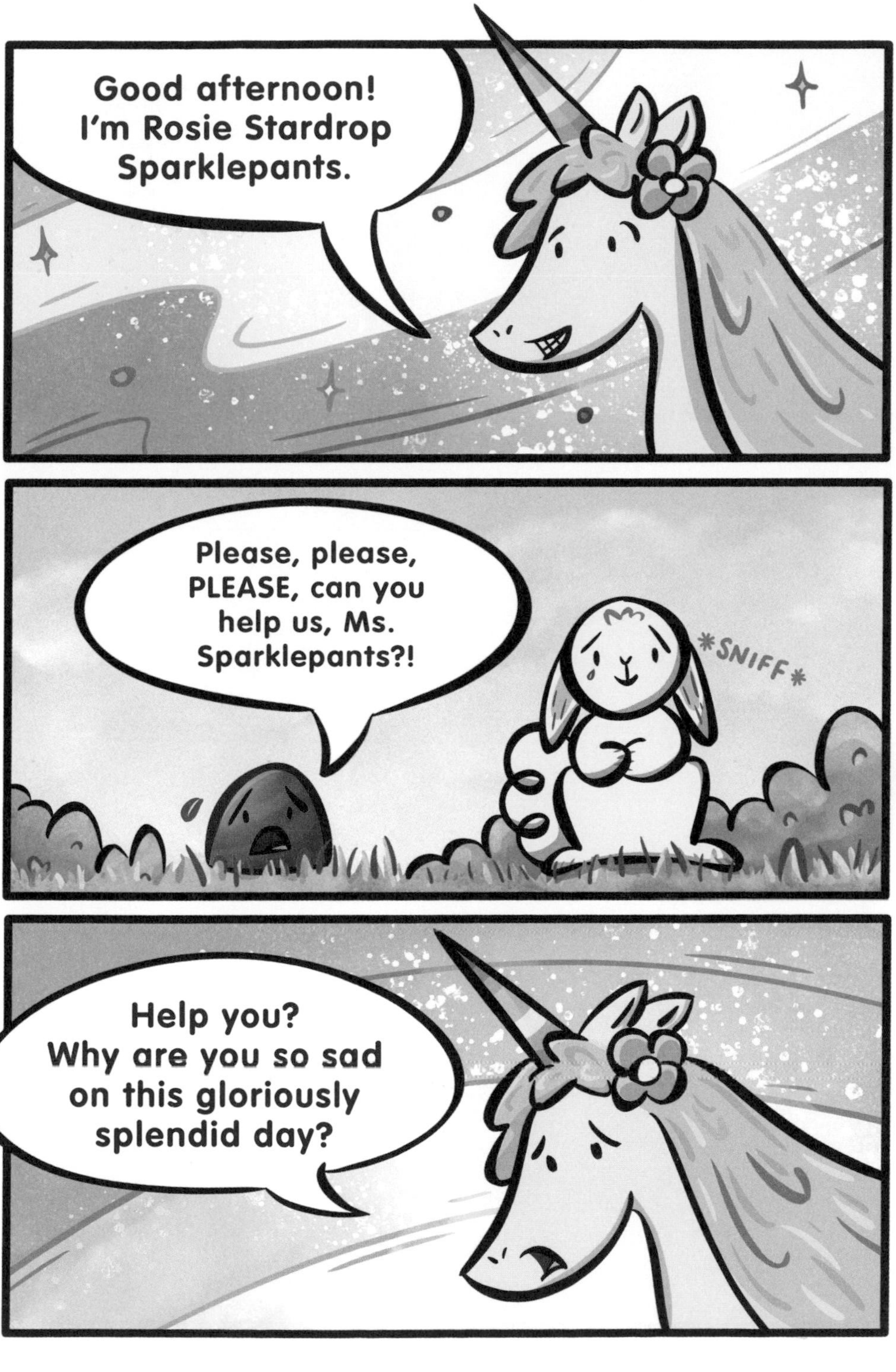
Good afternoon! I'm Rosie Stardrop Sparklepants.
Please, please, PLEASE, can you help us, Ms. Sparklepants?!
SNIFF
Help you? Why are you so sad on this gloriously splendid day?

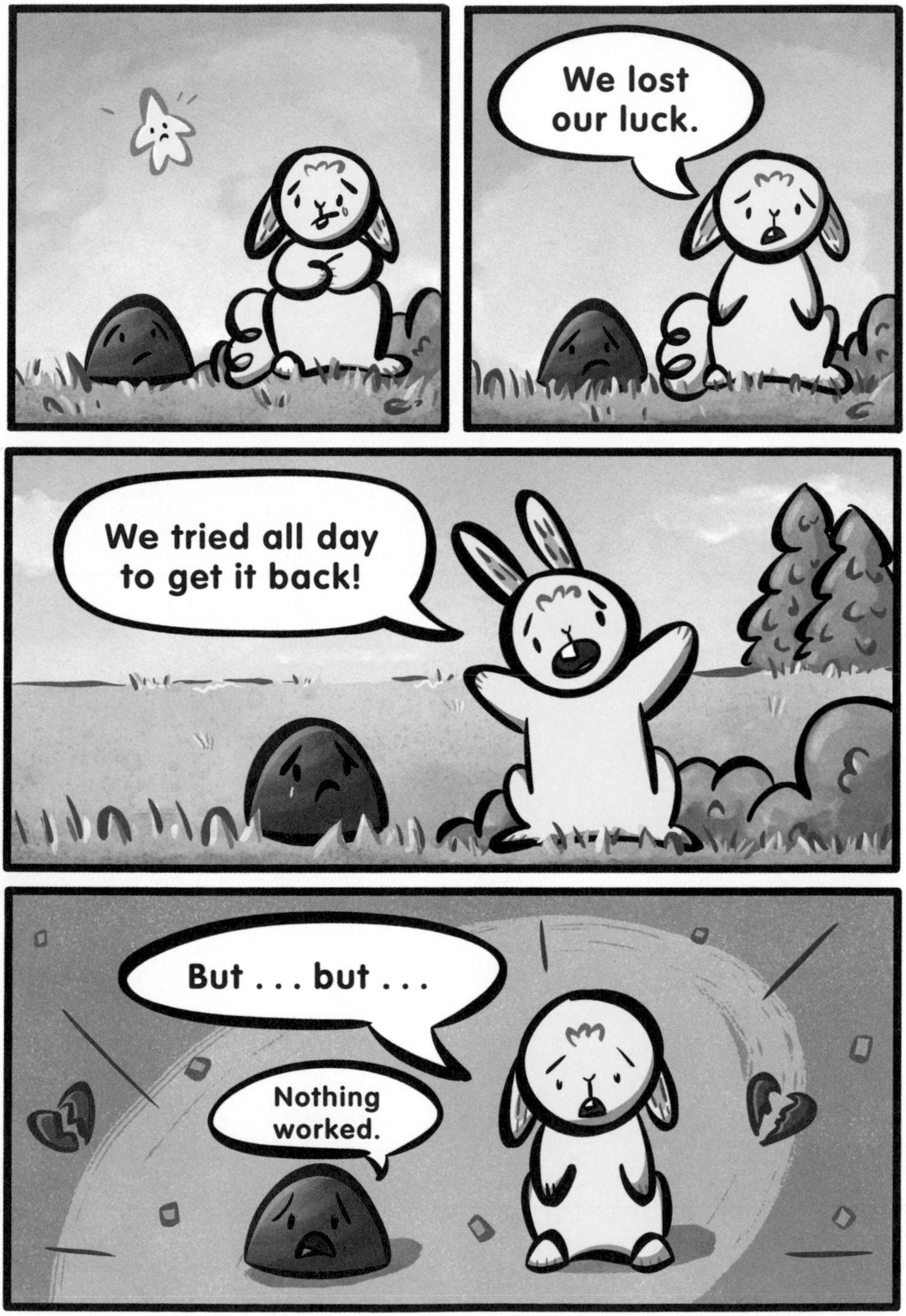
We lost our luck.
We tried all day to get it back!
But . . . but . . .
Nothing worked.

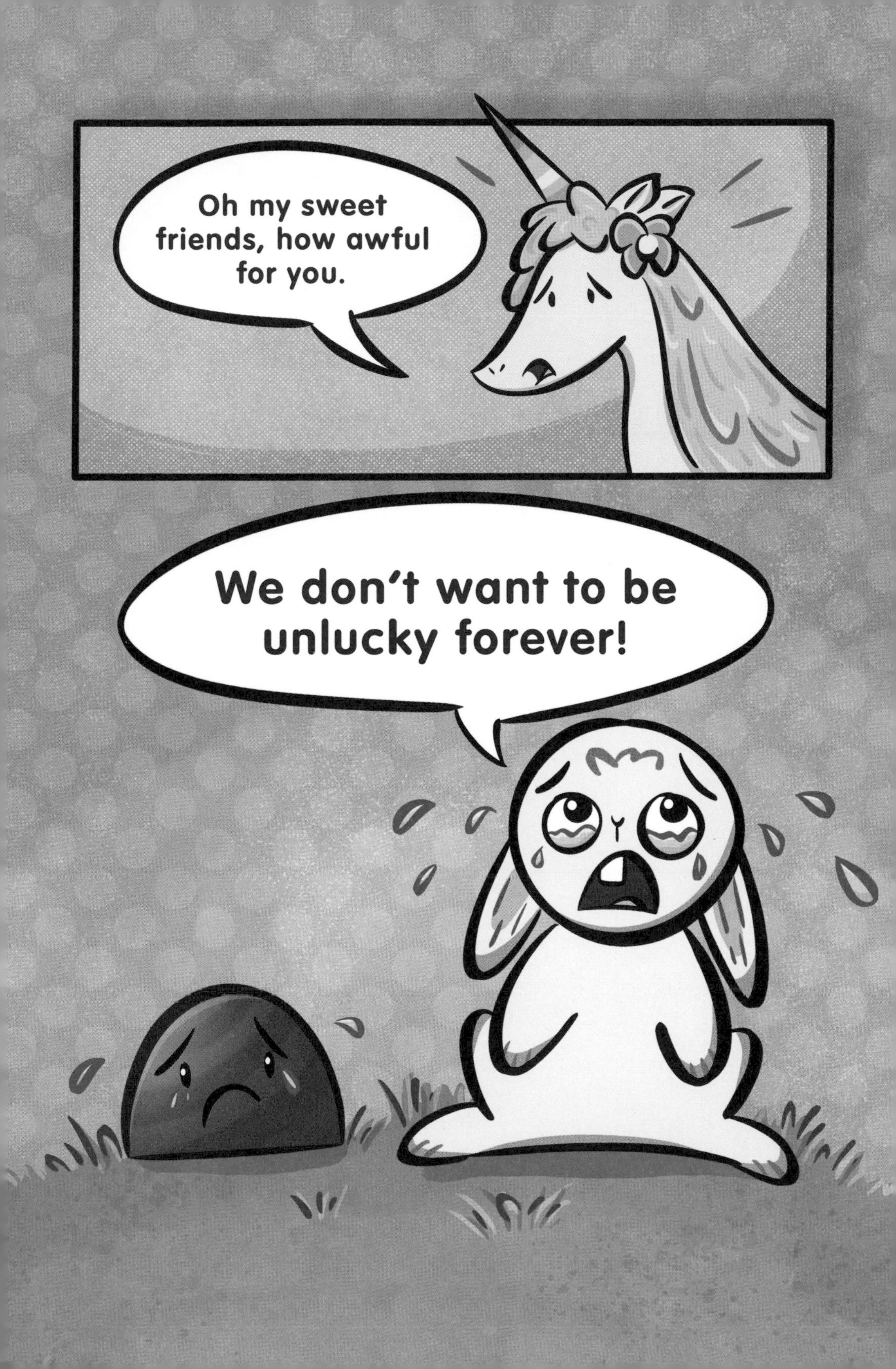
Oh my sweet friends, how awful for you.
We don't want to be unlucky forever!

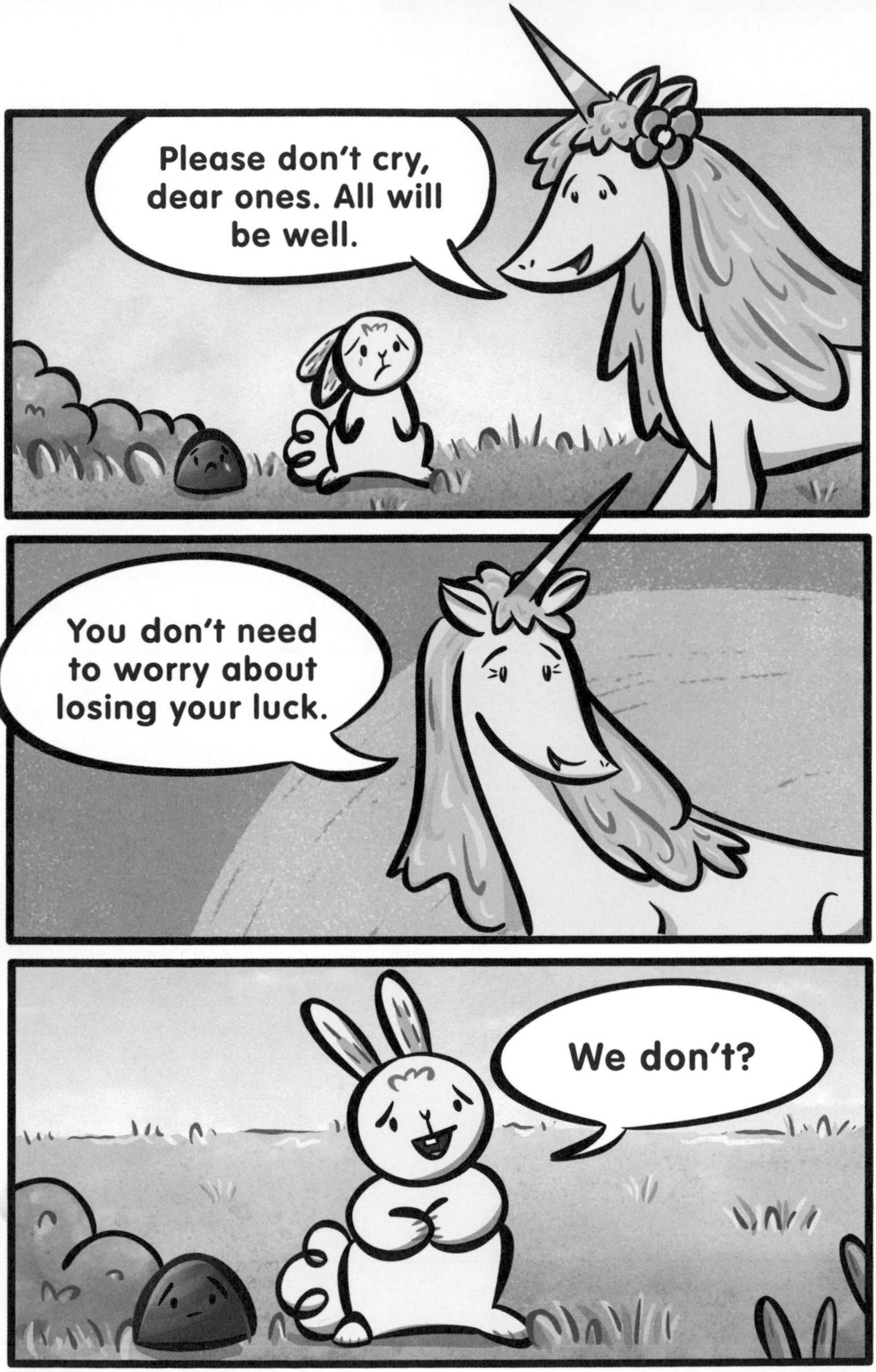
Please don't cry, dear ones. All will be well.
You don't need to worry about losing your luck.
We don't?

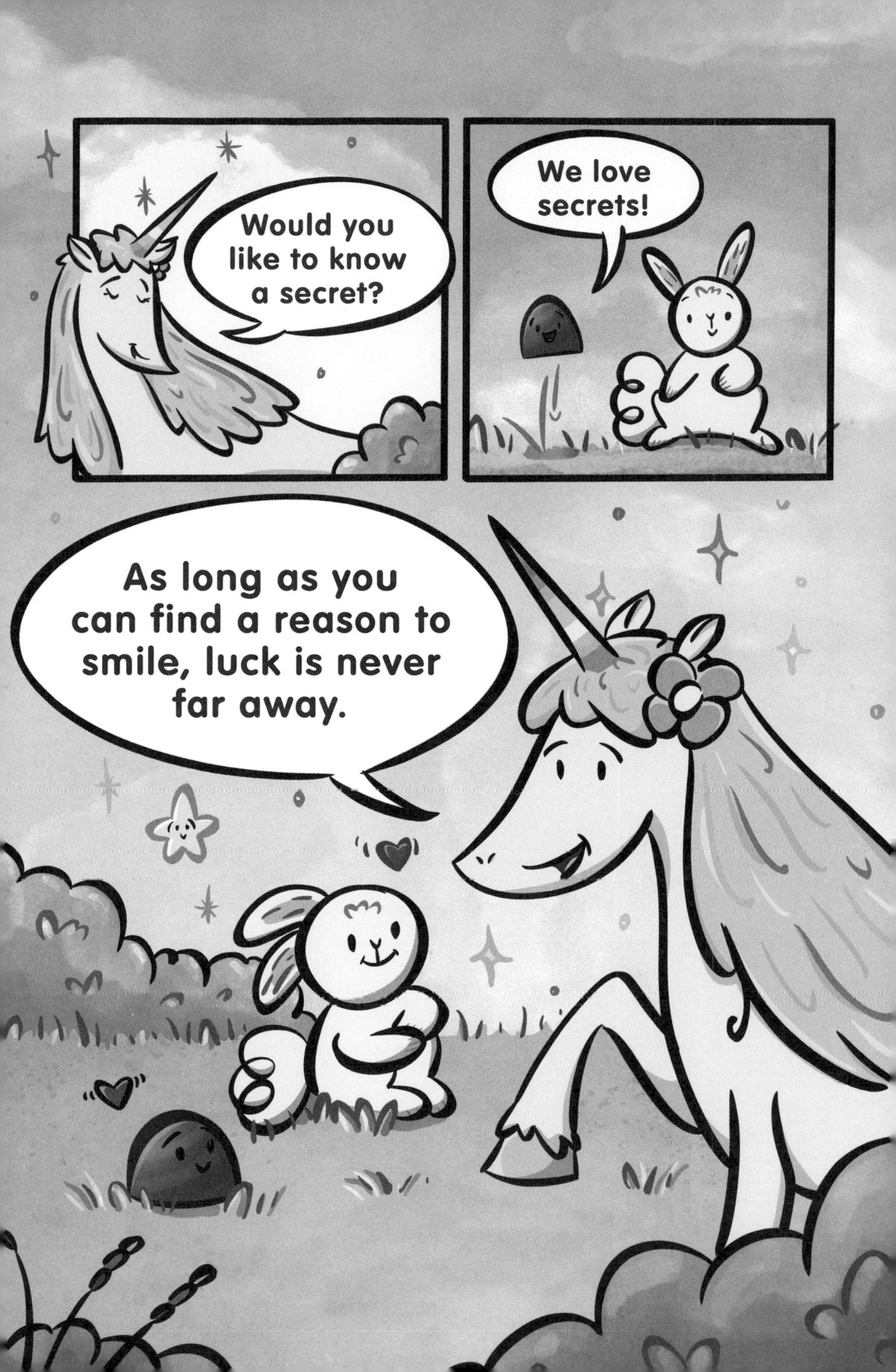
Would you like to know a secret?
We love secrets!
As long as you can find a reason to smile, luck is never far away.

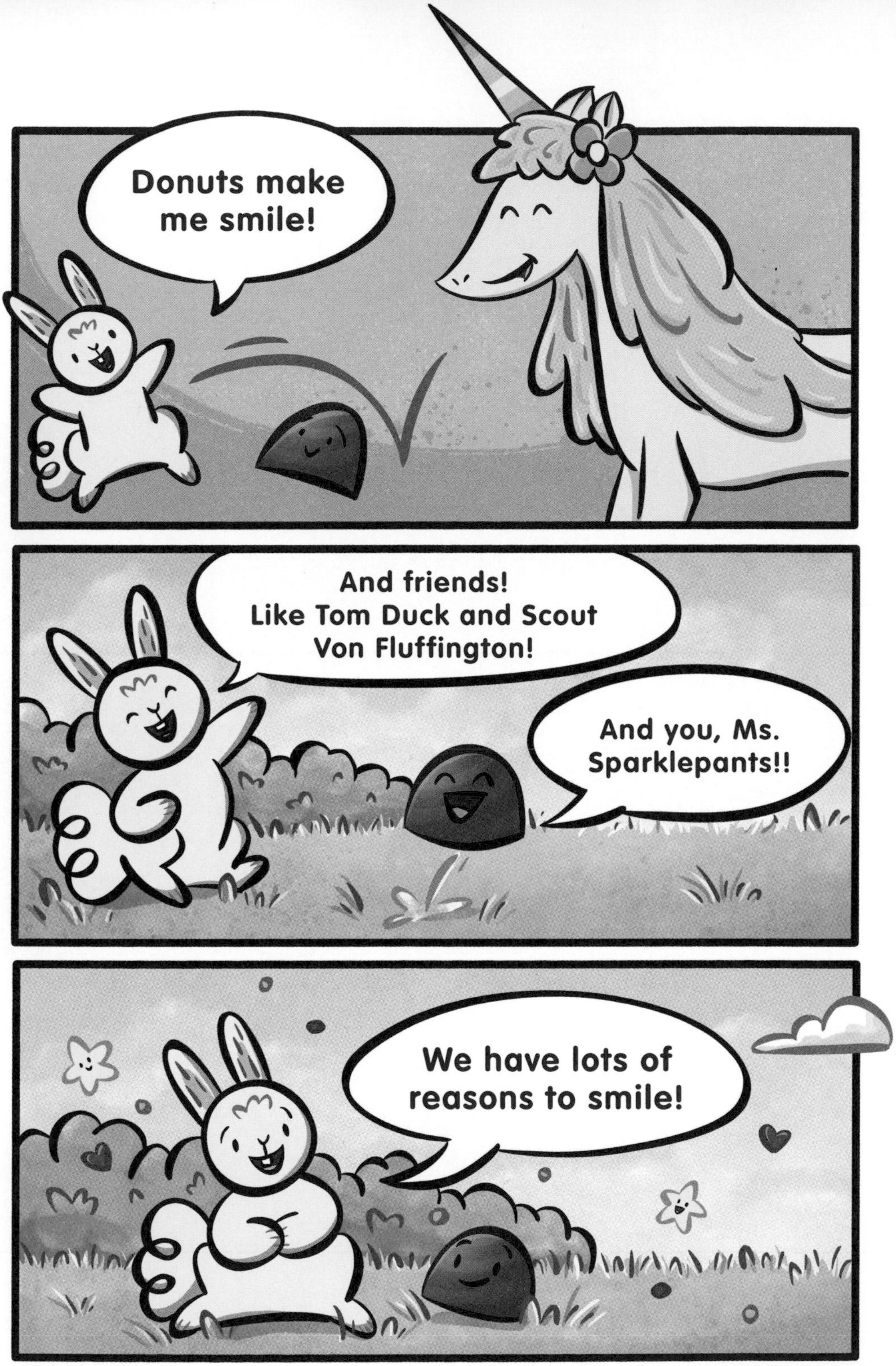
Donuts make me smile!
And friends! Like Tom Duck and Scout Von Fluffington!
And you, Ms. Sparklepants!!
We have lots of reasons to smile!

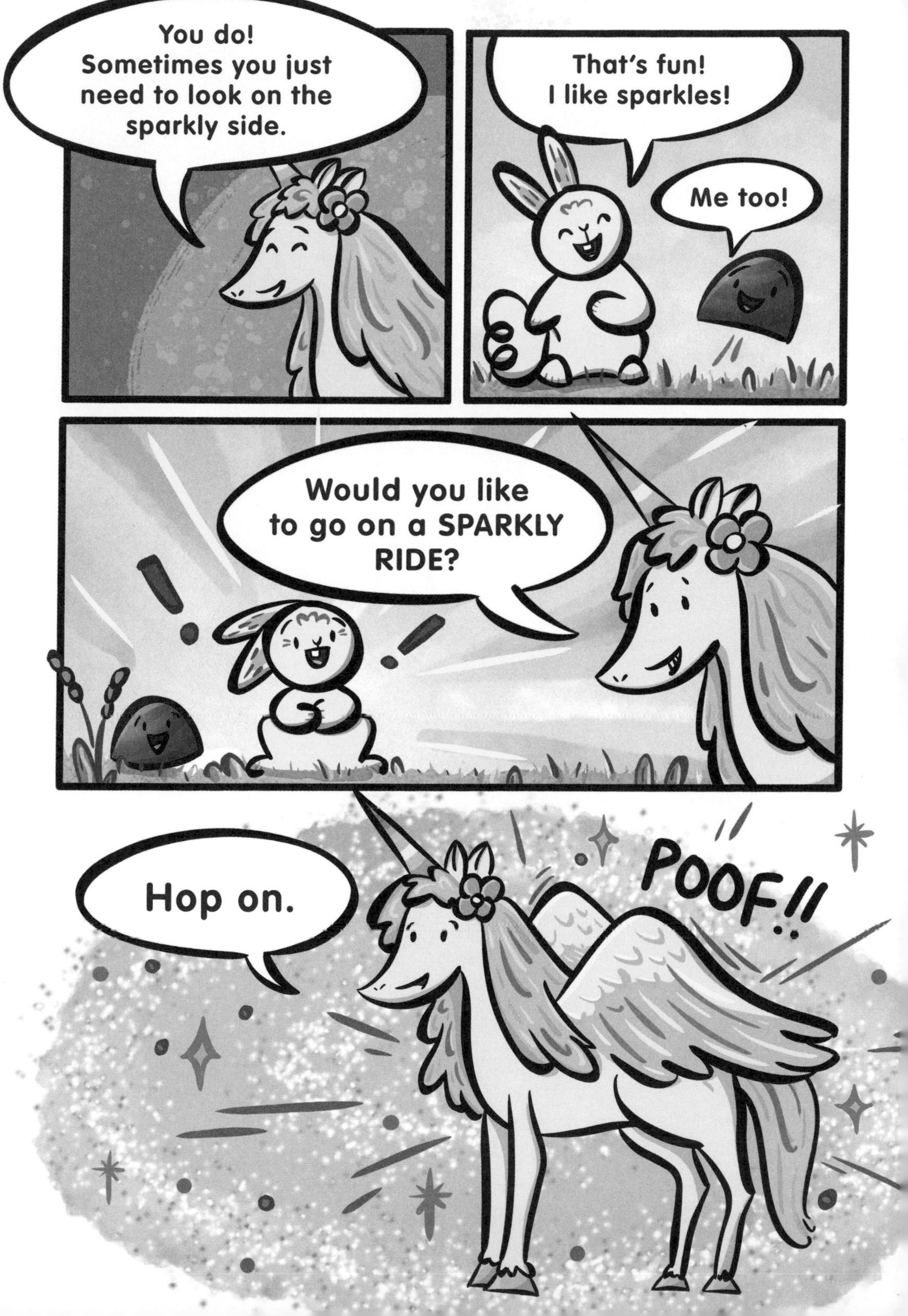
You do!
Sometimes you just need to look on the sparkly side.
That's fun!
I like sparkles!
Me too!
Would you like to go on a SPARKLY RIDE?
Hop on.
POOF!!

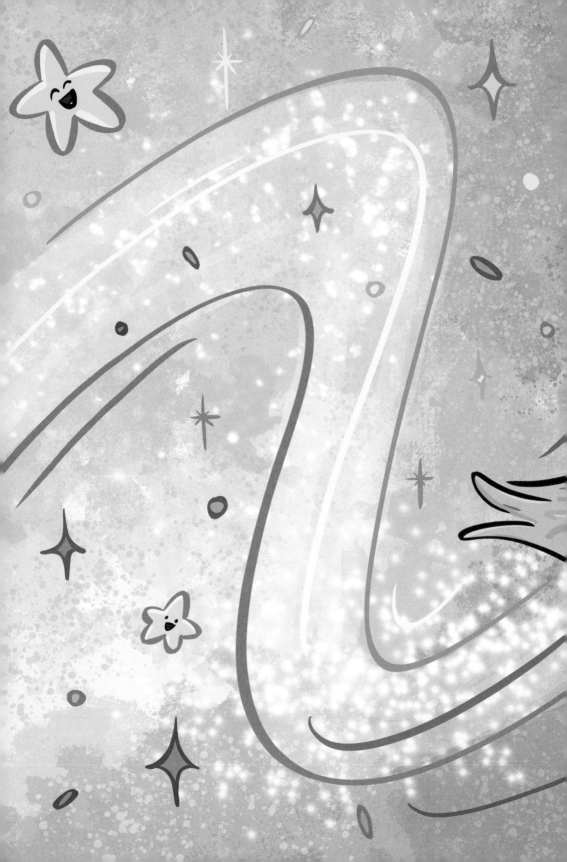

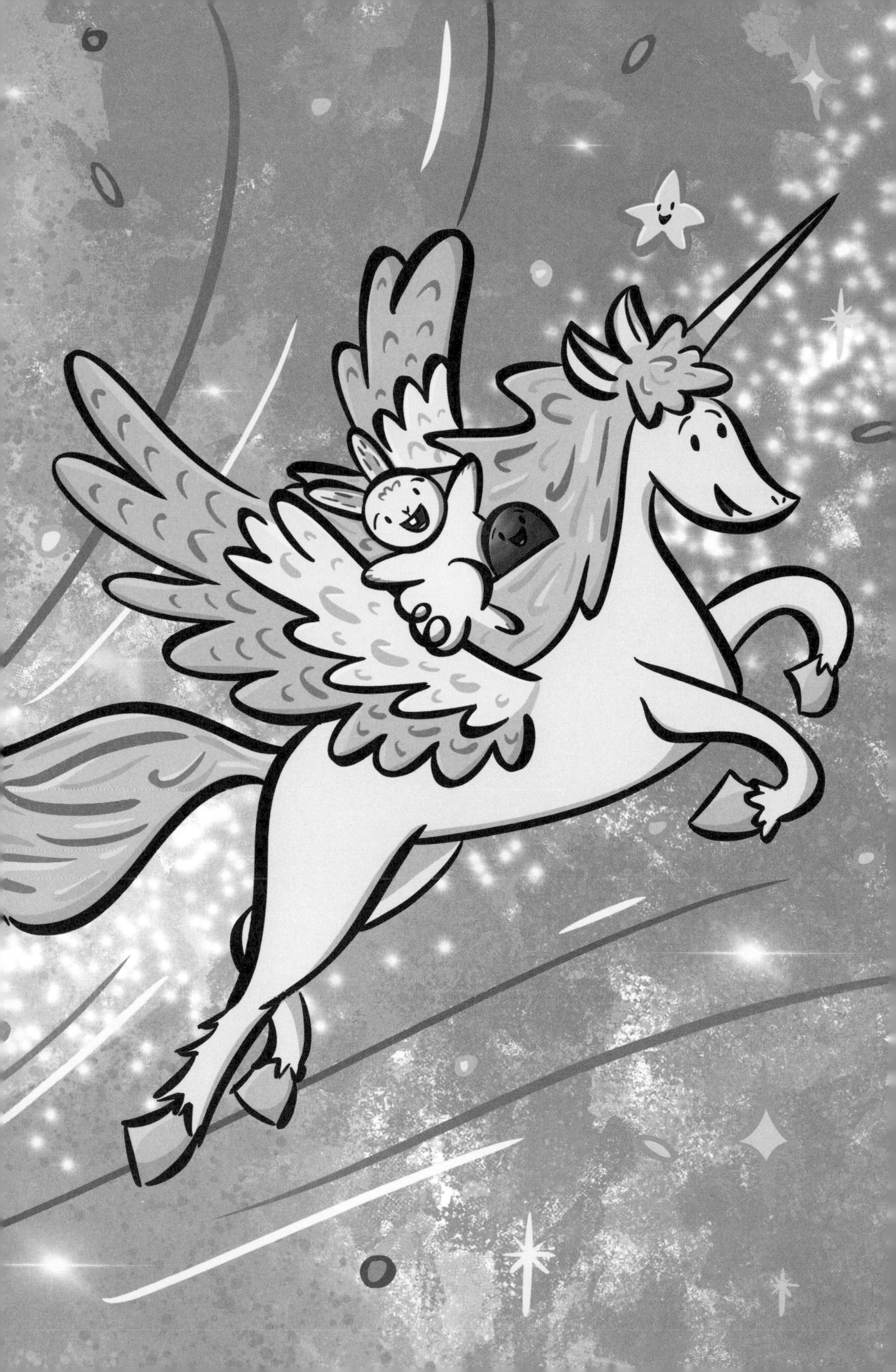

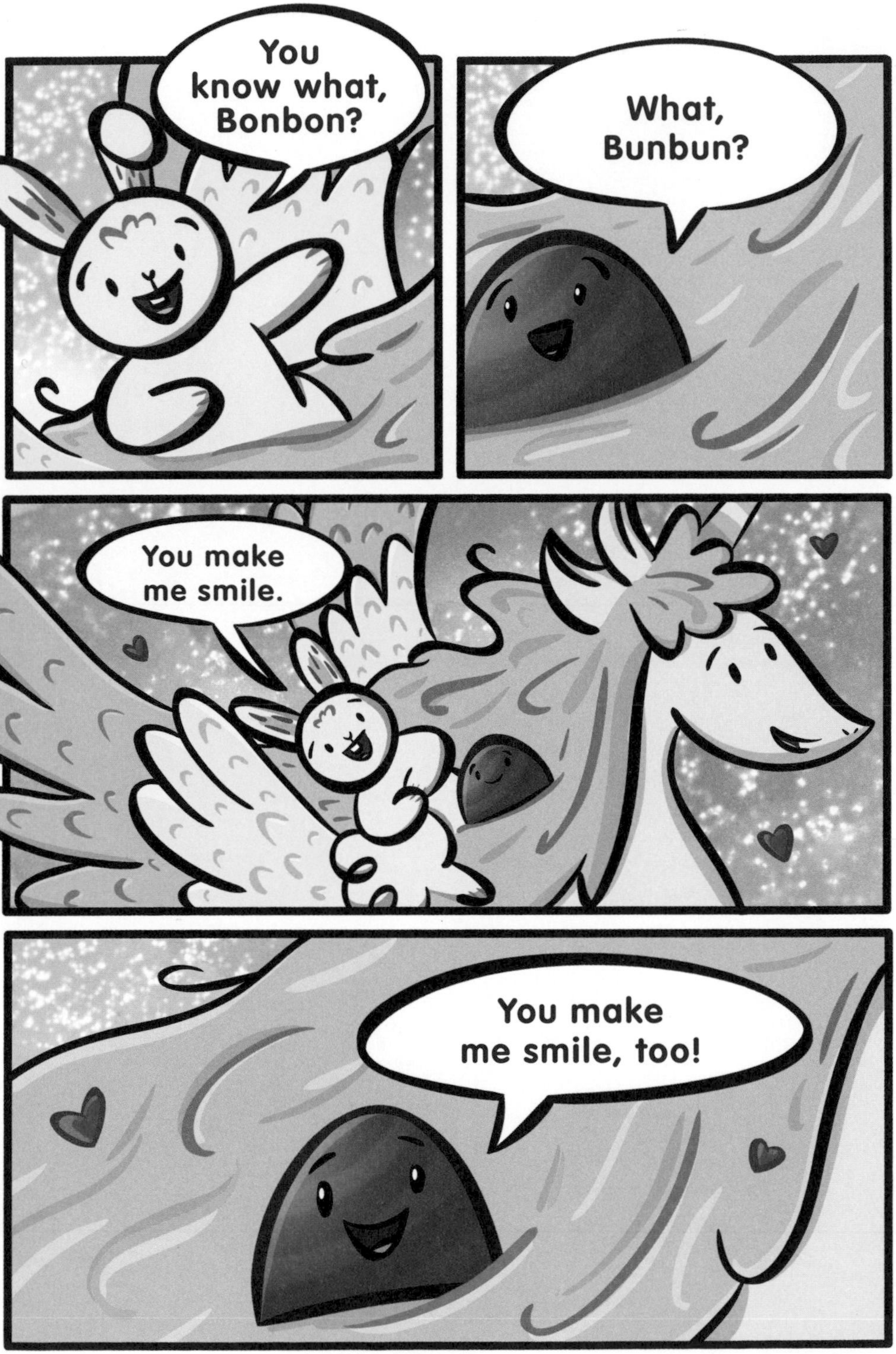
You know what, Bonbon?
What, Bunbun?
You make me smile.
You make me smile, too!

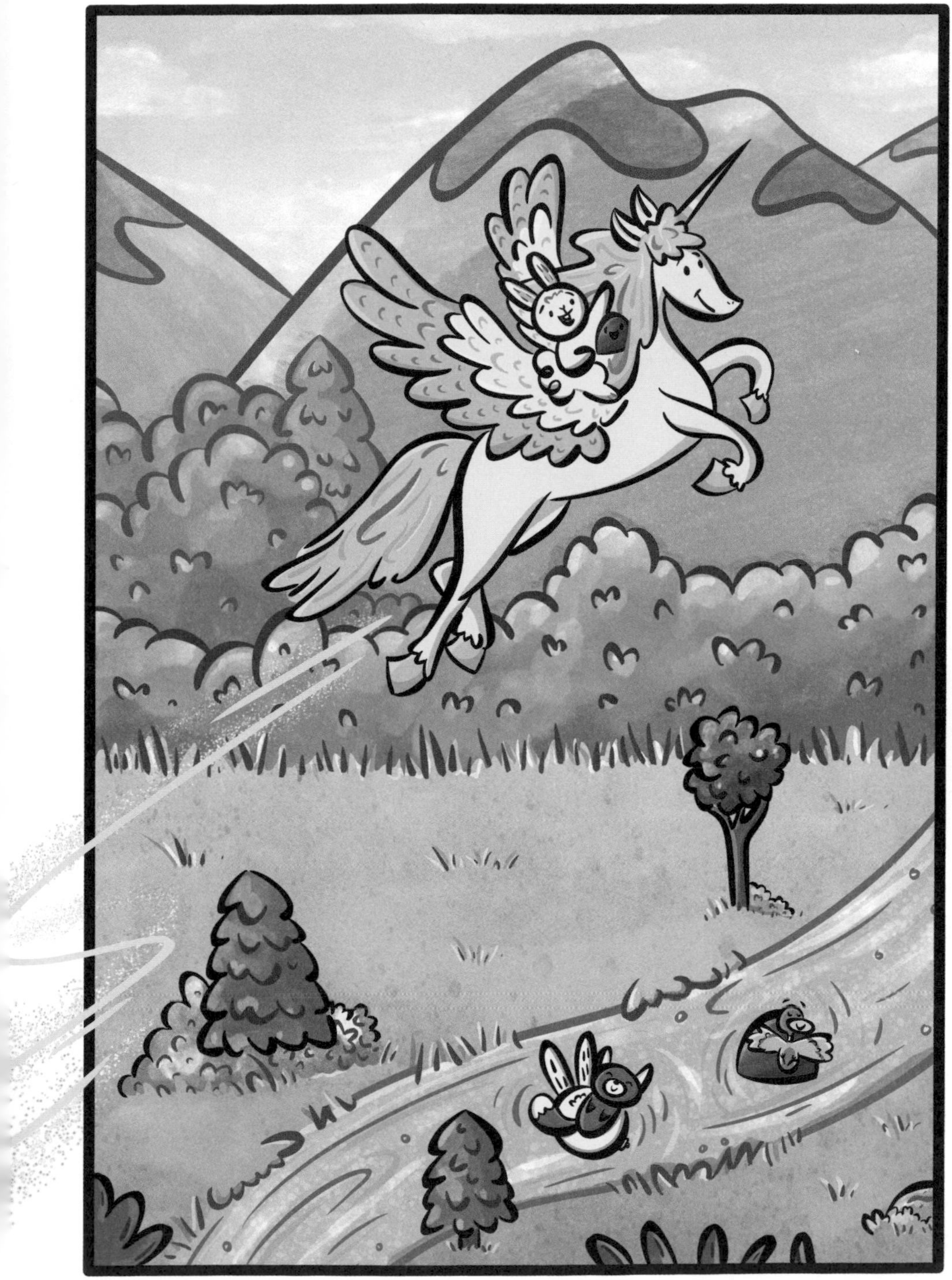

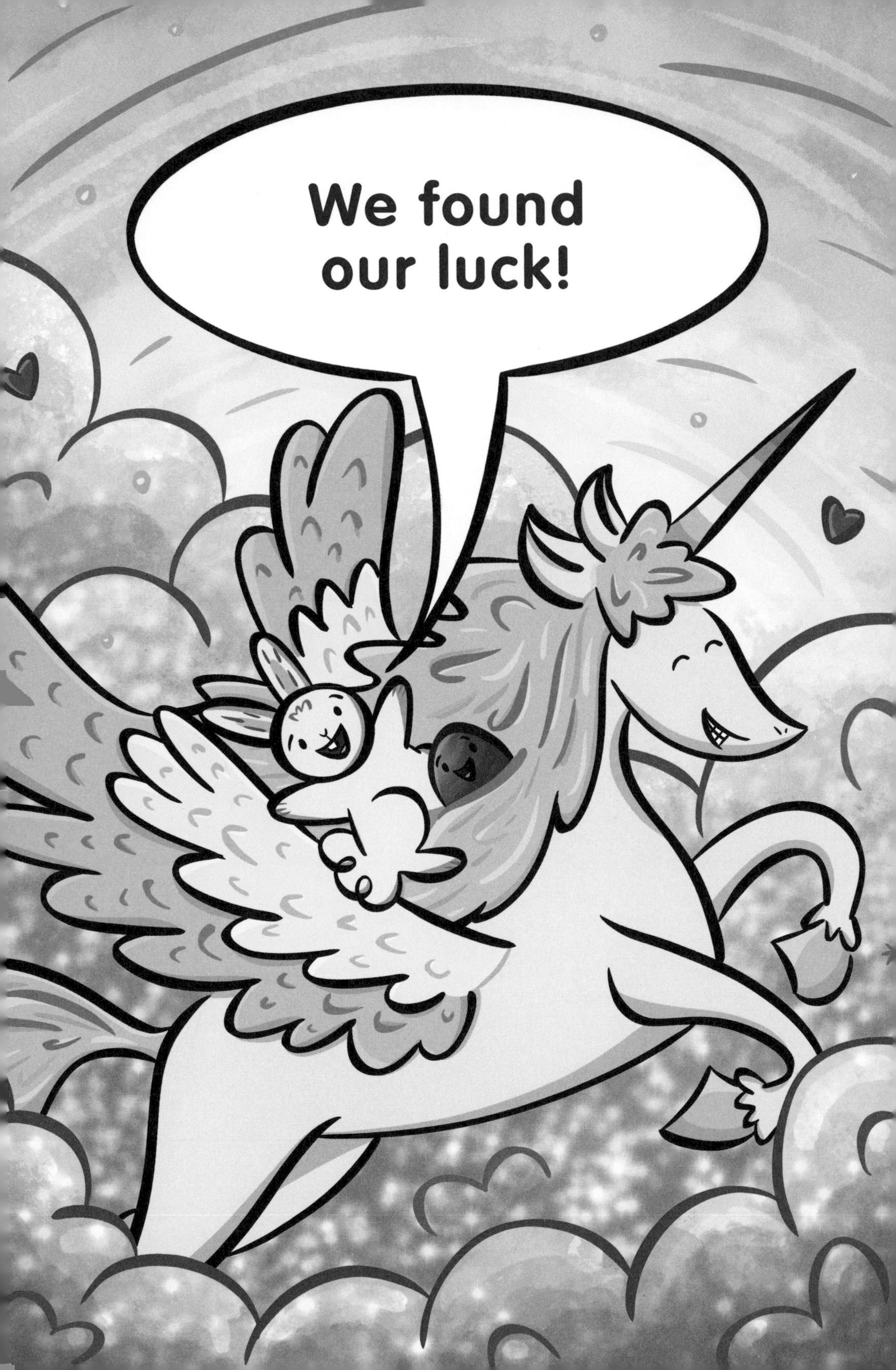
We found our luck!

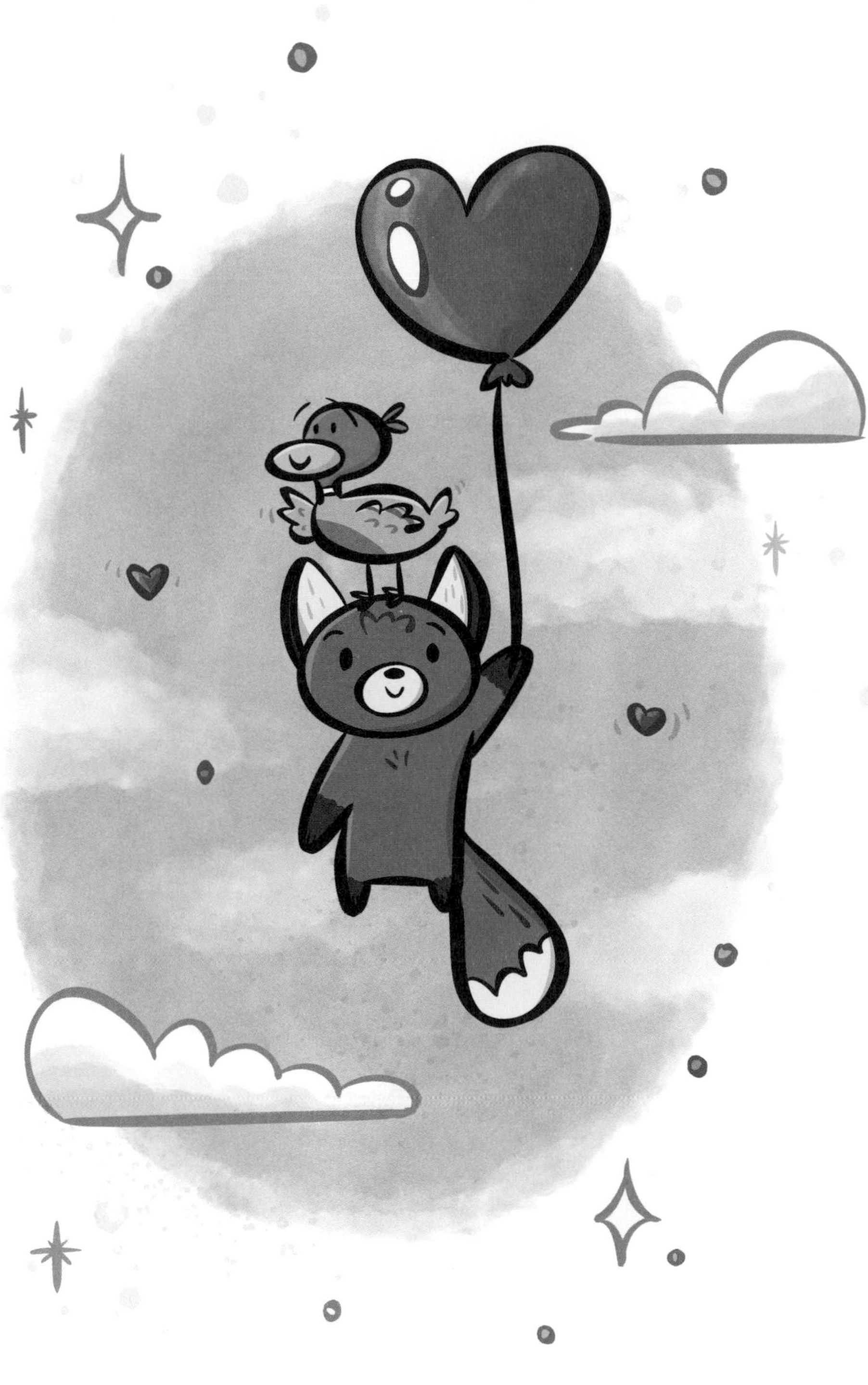

JESS KEATING is an award-winning author, cartoonist, and zoologist. She is the creator of over a dozen fiction and nonfiction books, including *Eat Your Rocks, Croc!*, *Shark Lady*, *Pink Is for Blobfish*, and the Elements of Genius middle-grade series. She lives in Ontario, Canada, where she's surrounded by books, bunnies, and bonbons. To learn more, tweet her @Jess_Keating, or visit jesskeatingbooks.com, where she shares behind-the-scenes work, resources for kids, and her weekly newsletter for creatives.